"You'r

And without so much as a by-your-leave, he unzipped his jacket, tugged the blanket open and stepped inside it with her. He urged her arms to slip around him inside his jacket, then wrapped his around her.

She sucked a sharp breath, about to protest instinctively. Then, "My God, you feel like a heater!"

"I've been nicely bundled up. And I'm willing to share."

All he did was share. She wanted him to bear down on her, make her forget by taking her right here, right now, still fully clothed…and a rocket trip to the stars would result.

"Getting warm?" he asked.

She had to struggle against impulses to answer. "Yes. Thank you." A mere breath of sound.

"Good. We need to keep you wrapped up."

In his arms? Oh, yes. But of course that wasn't what he meant.

"You were colder than you realized," he said. "I felt it."

And what else had he felt, she wondered.

★ ★ ★

Dear Reader,

Part of the fun of writing a book is doing research. While I've met folks who think contemporary novels don't need research, I don't agree. Yes, there are things we all know and are familiar with through daily life, but then there are the other things, the ones that send me to books and search engines.

Search engines are much better these days, and the wealth of information available on the web is wonderful. It wasn't always so. Not so very long ago, starting a new book meant buying books. I have shelves and shelves full of reference works that I'll never part with even if I never need them again. My house looks like a library.

These days I have to buy fewer reference books, but the challenge remains the same: not to trip myself up by making mistakes that will annoy those of you who know so much more than I do.

There's another challenge, too: I don't want all that research to appear on the pages in a way that you notice. It has to flow as seamlessly as possible into the story, because I want you to enjoy the story, not an interesting paragraph I found in a reference book. When you've spent hours or days researching something, it's sometimes hard to pare all that knowledge down to a simple toss-off in a sentence. But that's my job.

I hope you enjoy *The Rescue Pilot*, and I hope you don't notice the research. I also hope I didn't make a mistake.

Hugs,

Rachel

RACHEL LEE

The Rescue Pilot

ROMANTIC
SUSPENSE

Recycling programs
for this product may
not exist in your area.

ISBN-13: 978-0-373-27741-4

THE RESCUE PILOT

Printed in U.S.A.

Books by Rachel Lee

RACHEL LEE

was hooked on writing by the age of twelve, and practiced her craft as she moved from place to place all over the United States. This *New York Times* bestselling author now resides in Florida and has the joy of writing full-time.

Her bestselling Conard County series (see www.conardcounty.com) has won the hearts of readers worldwide, and it's no wonder, given her own approach to life and love. As she says, "Life is the biggest romantic adventure of all—and if you're open and aware, the most marvelous things are just waiting to be discovered." Readers can email Rachel at RachelLee@ConardCounty.com.

To all the quiet heroes who do whatever
is necessary to care for others.

Prologue

Thunder Mountain opened its snowy maw and swallowed the crashing plane. The business jet, its engines dead, not designed to glide without the assistance of power, descended almost like a stone, but the pilot struggled manfully.

The wild creatures, those not slumbering for winter, heard it come in, cutting through the air with a too-quiet but unnatural *whoosh,* heading for the only treeless space for miles. Those nearby froze and watched the thing slide, burying itself deeper in the snow as it went, metal screaming as it twisted, leaving a trail behind that would vanish quickly as the arriving blizzard blew mightily and dumped its heavy load. Then they turned and fled.

All fell silent. The flakes continued to swirl madly,

the wind to gust powerfully. Wise creatures found hiding places from the storm's fury.

And Thunder Mountain began to devour all the evidence of the crash.

Chapter 1

Chase Dakota stared at cockpit windscreens buried in snow, dirt, rocks and branches. Only the flickering light from his dying console allowed him to see anything at all. Moments later, to his relief, the emergency lights turned on again. Dim but essential.

For long seconds he didn't move, but instead listened. Listened to a world gone oddly silent, muffled by snow and the plane's own soundproofing. No screams reached him. That could be good, or very bad.

He was sweat-soaked from the effort of bringing this damn plane down. The instant the engines had cut out, he'd begun to fly a boulder not a bird, and his battle to optimize the aerodynamics and prevent a fatal dive had been Herculean. Hitting the mountain's downslope had been a boon.

Now he cut off the fuel pumps. Although they'd had a dramatic drop in fuel level, he couldn't be sure something else hadn't caused the dual flameout of his engines and that there might be more than fumes left. Next he switched off everything else that was nonessential now that they were no longer in the air. Mission accomplished.

He took just a moment to do a mental self-check. He wasn't aware of having lost consciousness at any point, but he might not have known it even if he had. Everything still seemed to be in working condition. Good.

He didn't have time for shock. He reached for the buckles of his harness and released them. His first priority was to check on his four passengers. Everything else could wait.

Even as he rose and stepped through the small cockpit, his feet told him the plane had been seriously bent on impact. But looking back through the cabin as he pulled aside the accordion door, he saw with relief that the rest of the plane seemed to be intact. All of it. That meant his passengers were still with him. All of them.

At first all he could hear was panicked breathing. Then a familiar voice said, "That was a helluva landing, Chase."

Billy Joe Yuma. An old buddy.

"Not my preferred type," Chase managed, working his way back through the narrow-bodied business jet. "Anyone hurt?"

"I'm fine," Yuma said. "So's Wendy."

"Ms. Campbell?"

"I…think I'm okay. My sister…"

"I'm checking right now."

He passed the three people, still tightly buckled into their seats, and made his way to the small bedroom in the tail where the sick woman lay. He'd insisted that she be strapped in, overriding the Campbell woman's objections, and never had he been gladder that he'd been willing to go toe-to-toe over something. He grabbed a flashlight from a wall compartment as he passed the small bathroom, and flicked it on.

He saw her, still strapped in place, still too thin to be believed, but blinking. Awake. Aware. Panic filling her face.

"It's okay," he said. "We came down in one piece."

"Fire?" she asked weakly.

"Nope. None. You're going to be okay." An easy, hopeful lie. At this point he didn't have the foggiest idea just how bad this was. He was counting the good things right now, and the good things were that his passengers were alive and his plane intact enough not to present additional problems.

He paused, feeling the aircraft shift a bit as if the wind banged on its side. A quiet groan of metal answered, but nothing more.

"My sister?" the woman on the bed asked, her voice faint.

"She's fine. Everyone's okay. I'll send her back, all right?"

He didn't even have to do that. As soon as he turned around, he was face-to-face with the imperious young woman who had hired him to take her and her sister to Minneapolis. If she weren't so damn bossy, she'd have been an attractive Celtic beauty, with her black hair and deep blue eyes. "Cait," she said.

"She's asking for you."

He stepped into the W.C. to give her room to pass. Then he headed back up the aisle. With every step he felt the torture the plane had gone through as it had slid along the mountain slope. The deep snow had helped, but it wasn't enough to completely shield the plane from the ground underneath, especially boulders. This baby would never fly again.

But now it had one last duty: to help them survive. Glancing out the portholes that weren't yet fully covered by snow told him the blizzard conditions he'd been flying above had begun to reach them. Rescue lay a long way down the road of time and this mountain.

He sat in an empty seat facing Wendy and Billy Joe Yuma. He'd known them both most of his life—the advantage of living in a small town. And he knew he was going to need them both now. They belonged to Conard County's emergency-response team, Wendy as chief flight nurse, Yuma (he hated to be called Billy Joe) as the primary rescue chopper pilot.

Wendy, now a gorgeous redhead of nearly forty, was much younger than her husband. Yuma had learned to fly choppers in Vietnam, and despite the years maintained an ageless appearance. Or maybe he'd done all his aging during the years of war, and afterward when he'd lived in these very mountains with a bunch of vets who couldn't shake their PTSD enough to live around other people.

"You're sure you're both okay?" he asked now.

"Believe it," Wendy answered.

"Been through worse," Yuma replied, "and walked away."

Chase didn't doubt that for a minute. He, too, had flown for the military.

"I'm gonna need you both," he said frankly. "We've got a really sick woman in the tail we need to take care of, Wendy. And Yuma, I need you to help me find out what still works, and how we're going to cope with this blizzard."

He received two answering nods, and both unbuckled their seat belts.

"I'll go back and find out what's going on," Wendy said. "Why do I think it's going to need more than a first aid kit?"

"Because I was supposed to fly them on to the hospital in Minnesota."

"Oh." Even in the poor light he could see Wendy's face darken. "That doesn't sound good." She rose, slipped past the two of them and headed to the rear of the plane.

Chase turned back to Yuma. "We need to make sure we can get one of the exit doors open, and keep it clear. And a walk-around would be good before we get buried any deeper."

"Agreed. Then we'll check the electronics. But first things first."

As they began to pull on their outdoor gear, Chase noted that the air inside was already becoming stale. The downside of having an airtight shelter. He was going to have to figure out how to exchange the cabin air without freezing them to death.

He gave a small shake of his head. As Yuma said, first things first.

Aurora Campbell, known as Rory to family and friends, sat on the edge of her sister's bed in the rear of the plane and clasped her hand as tightly as she dared. Her sister had grown so thin from her lymphoma and the treatments for the cancer that holding her hand was like holding the delicate bones of a small bird.

She hoped her face betrayed nothing of her terror. She'd deal with that later when she gave their pilot whatfor. Right now she only wanted to calm Cait.

"The hard part is over," she lied reassuringly. "Hey, Cait, we were just in a plane crash but we're still in one piece. What are the odds, huh?"

Cait managed a weak smile. Even that simple expression seemed like it wearied her. "Yeah," she said, her voice little more than a whisper. "And people will come to help."

"Yes, they will." Despite the blizzard raging outside, despite the fact that she was fairly certain they were in the middle of nowhere. "And I've got enough medications to hold you until they do." Four days' worth. She had thought she wouldn't need even that much, because Cait had been slated for immediate admission at the hospital they were going to. Had been going to until this freaking jet had crashed on a mountainside in what was starting to look like a damn blizzard.

But for now she shoved her frustration, fear and fury to the background. "Need anything? Maybe I can rustle up some soup…." God, she hadn't even thought about that yet, either. Did this plane have anything on it besides snacks and liquor? Anything that didn't require a microwave to cook it? Because she suspected that was one of the things that probably wouldn't work now.

She didn't know much about planes, but she knew most of their electricity was generated by their engines. And this plane had no engines anymore.

"No," Cait sighed. "As long as we're okay…I just want to sleep a bit."

Rory reached out and stroked the pale fuzz that was all that remained on Cait's head. "You do that." Cait was sleeping more and more of the time. Her heart squeezed, but moments later as Cait slipped away into sleep, she rose and walked out of the little bedroom.

The other woman passenger was waiting for her.

Wendy, Rory seemed to remember. On such small business jets, it was hard not to at least exchange introductions before takeoff.

"I'm a nurse," Wendy said. "Let's sit and talk a bit about your sister so I can help."

"You can't help her," Rory said brusquely. "I have her medicines. What she needs is a hospital, a clinical trial on a new drug. Doesn't look likely right now, does it?" Then she eased past Wendy and returned to her seat, blindly watching the snow build up outside the small window.

She hardly even paid attention to the two men who were forward in the cabin, working to open the exterior door behind the cockpit. She noted that the air was getting heavy, but at the moment she wasn't worried about that.

All she was worried about was Cait, and right at this moment, with the world outside invisible in swirling snow, she was fairly certain there wasn't a damn thing she could do. And she hated, absolutely *hated*, being helpless.

Wendy didn't give her long to sit in hopeless solitude. The woman came forward and sat in the seat facing her. "Cancer?" Wendy asked.

"Non-Hodgkins lymphoma. Aggressive, this time." The words were painful, but she'd never been one to shy away from telling it like it was. No matter how much it hurt.

"This time?" Wendy's voice was gentle.

Rory almost sighed, realizing that she could either choose to be unutterably rude and say nothing, or just dump it out there and shut this woman up. She decided on the latter. "She went into remission four years ago. Unfortunately, she didn't tell me she had a relapse five

months ago. I was in Mexico, and she didn't tell me."
That hurt as much as anything.

"So you came home to find her like this? Why
wouldn't she tell you?"

"She'd given up," Rory said. "Her husband dumped
her the minute he heard and moved in with another
woman. Kinda cuts out your heart, don't you think?"

"It would."

Rory heard the sympathy in Wendy's voice, but she
didn't want sympathy. Sympathy didn't help. All it did
was make her want to cry. She didn't answer.

"You have medication for her."

Rory finally looked at her, her eyes burning.
"Enough for four days. More than enough for a freaking four- or five-hour flight from Seattle to Minneapolis. Only that's not happening, is it?"

To her credit, Wendy didn't offer any false cheer.
"What's she on?"

"Immunosuppressants. Some other drugs. She's been
through radiation, obviously. But as I said, the disease
is aggressive."

"So you're pinning your hopes on a clinical trial of
something new?"

"Yes. I was." That *was* sounded final. But right now
everything felt final.

"They've got some great stuff now, I hear, but I'm
not up on the disease." She leaned forward and laid her
hand over Rory's.

Rory wanted to jerk back, but she couldn't because
that touch somehow didn't offend her. Maybe because
she needed not to feel entirely alone. "That's what they
tell me."

Wendy nodded. "The important thing is to keep her
going right now. Food. Warmth. Keep her resistance up.

I'll help every way I can. But I promise you, I'm part of the Conard County emergency-response team. As soon as this weather lets up, they're going to pull out all the stops to find us."

"Because you're here?"

"Because all of us are here. And we're damn good at what we do."

"How do you know we aren't someplace else?"

"Because Chase was going to drop us at the Conard County Airport on the way to Minnesota. You knew that, right?"

Rory nodded. "A brief fueling stop."

"Well, my husband was looking out the window as we came in. He said this is Thunder Mountain, maybe sixty miles out of town."

It was a slender lifeline indeed, but for once in her life, Rory was willing to grab it. What else did she have?

Turning her head, closing the conversation, she gazed out a window that snow rapidly covered, and fought down the rage, panic and tears.

The exit door behind the cockpit also served as steps. The fact that it opened out and down should have made it easier to move. But the plane's shape had been torqued by the crash, and things weren't meeting the way they used to. And the steps themselves, carpeted for that extra bit of luxury, hampered the effort to shove.

"Maybe we should try the rear exit," Yuma said, wiping sweat from his brow.

"I'd rather not open the door back there if I can avoid it. Any cold air we let in—and there'll be quite a bit of it—is going to hit our sick passenger first. I'd rather let it in as far from her as possible."

"Good point. Well, I doubt the snow is the problem."

"Not hardly," Chase agreed. "Not yet. Not with this."

But the snow was a problem all right, one that promised to grow even bigger in the next few hours. "We've got to get out," he said again. "Find out what our condition is, whether we've got anything else to worry about. And we're going to need to build a fire to heat food."

"In this?" Yuma cocked a brow. "That's always fun."

"I have plenty of alcohol onboard."

Yuma chuckled. "Imagine starting a fire with Chivas. Or Jack."

"I just hope it works. Alcohol burns cold."

"A handful of pine needles" was all Yuma said.

"Sure. I see tons of them out there." But Chase knew that even though the snow buried them, finding them wouldn't be the most difficult task they'd face. But first this damn door. Preferably in a way that wouldn't leave it permanently open to the cold.

"You know," he said as he and Yuma again put their shoulders to the door, "I should have painted this damn plane chartreuse or international orange."

"By tomorrow I don't think it'll matter if it were covered in blinking neon lights."

Chase paused, wiping his own brow. "Yeah. It probably won't."

"Transponder?" Billy Joe asked as they pushed again.

"Damned if I know right now. My instruments were acting like twinkle lights. But first things first. The transponder isn't exactly going to get much attention at the moment."

"That's a fact."

"At the very least we've got to check our situation, make sure we don't slide farther, and then get some hot

soup and coffee going. *Then* I'll worry about everything else."

"Agreed."

On the count of three, both men shoved again, and
this time the door opened. Not far, just a couple of
inches at the top, but enough for Chase to see the problem. One of the heavy-duty locking bolts hadn't slid
fully back and it ripped at the door, tearing a small hole
but not enough to cause any heartache.

"I need a sledgehammer," Chase muttered. And he
needed it right now, because he wasn't going to go outside and leave that door open, freezing everyone in the
plane.

He pulled up a service panel in the floor and went
hunting. There it was, a heavy-duty hammer. He hadn't
ever needed it, but you never knew. He carried a lot of
items just for that reason. If he'd learned one thing in
the military, it was to be prepared for just about any
situation. What you dismissed as unnecessary could
wind up costing you a whole lot…like your life.

Yuma leaned back while Chase started hammering
on the locking bolt.

"Do you have to make so much noise?" the Campbell woman said sharply. "My sister…"

"Is going to freeze to death if I can't close this door,
okay?"

He didn't have to look at her because he could hear
the snap of her jaws closing just before he banged again
with the hammer.

To his vast relief, it only took a half-dozen blows.
He tossed the hammer back in the hatch, closed it and
then faced the door with Yuma again. Already the plane
was cooling down, but the fresher air was welcome.

They counted to three again and shoved. This time

the door flew all the way down to the packed snow beneath. Another scarcely acknowledged fear slipped away from Chase's mind. They weren't trapped inside. They had a functioning door.

The two men scrambled out quickly over the horizontal steps, which were useless at this angle, then shoved the door up behind them, leaving it open the tiniest crack.

Outside the world looked like a snow globe gone mad. Wind whipped them viciously, howling its fury, and the flakes were becoming icy needles. Chase ignored the discomfort, all his attention focused on finding out how the plane was situated. He didn't want to learn the hard way that they were on the lip of another slide and some little thing could set it off.

He headed straight for the plane's nose. In this heavy snow, it was hard to see very far. He could make out only the faintest of gray shadows of trees around the clearing, but as he approached the front, he saw with relief that there were trees not very far ahead of them. Maybe a hundred, two hundred feet at most. Thick foresting that would stop them if they slid, no dark shadow indicating a deep gorge in the way. Thank God.

The nose was completely buried and he left it that way. Every bit of insulation would do them good until this blizzard passed, cutting the wind, keeping the inside temperature up.

But he felt something very close to sorrow as he walked back along the plane's length. Even with deepening snowdrifts he could see buckled metal on the fuselage, and that the engines had vanished from under the wings somewhere upslope, leaving behind their twisted pylons. Any fuel that was left would be seeping into the snow from broken lines, but he couldn't see any melting to indicate it.

God, what had happened? He hadn't had time to wonder before. He'd gone from half-full tanks to empty so fast it had seemed almost impossible. His fuel pumps must have been spewing precious liquid as fast as they could from somewhere. Just where he wouldn't be able to tell now.

He'd had the damn thing overhauled and checked out last week. That's why he'd been in Seattle. All he could think now was that some mechanic somewhere had failed to do something right. Make some connection. Tighten some clamp, whatever. Somewhere between pumps and engines, there had been a critical failure.

By the time he'd known things were going wrong, they'd been over the mountains with a storm catching up. At forty thousand feet, that was no big deal, but it sure cut his options. He'd had no choice but to hope they'd make it to the Conard County Airport. There was nothing closer that hadn't already been closed by the storm.

He supposed he ought to get down on his knees and thank God they were in one piece. But right now he wasn't feeling all that thankful. He was feeling furious, and worried. Most especially worried about that sick woman in the back of his plane.

Chapter 2

Rory had added more blankets to cover Cait as the cabin temperature dropped a bit because of the opening and closing of the cabin door. She was grateful the air felt fresher now, but worried, too. How were they supposed to keep warm?

Cait barely stirred as Rory tucked blankets around her all the way up to her ears. A knit stocking cap would probably be good, she thought, since Cait didn't have enough hair left to keep her head warm.

She went out to ask Wendy about it. Maybe the other woman had one.

"Actually, I do," Wendy said. "And I'm glad to tell you it's in the overhead bin. Let me get it out. Didn't you bring something like that for when you got to Minnesota?"

"An ambulance was going to meet us. I wasn't expecting Cait to be exposed at all."

Wendy nodded as she rose to open one of the overhead bins. She wore a baggy sweater and jeans, and a very sensible pair of work boots. Just like Rory herself. Accustomed as she was to being on work sites, Rory dolled up only for business meetings, and this trip hadn't qualified for that.

"What about you?" Wendy spoke as she fought with the bin door, at last managing to yank it open.

"I have a parka I dug out before we left."

"Good. I don't usually carry spares of those."

Wendy pulled a thick-knit cap out of a leather duffel and passed it to her. "There you go."

"Thank you so much!"

Wendy smiled, and the expression reached her eyes. "Hey, we're all in this together."

Cait murmured quietly as Rory put the stocking cap on her, but then settled back into sleep. Rory stood looking down at her sister, wishing that for just a few moments she could see that spark again in Cait's expression, but it had vanished long before Rory got home.

Tears pricked at her eyes, but she couldn't afford to let them fall. Not now, not ever. She had to remain strong for Cait's sake, no matter how tough it got. And right now it was tough. All her worst imaginings for Cait's future had just been compounded by a plane crash in the wilderness. In a storm.

Sometimes she thought the gods enjoyed a laugh at human expense. If so, they must be finding this all hilarious.

Time. There was so little time for Cait now. And this accident was eating away at it like a miserable rat. Just enough meds for four days. Then what? Not that the meds were doing much but holding the beast at bay, and not doing a very good job at that. In the days since she'd gotten back to Seattle and had gathered the information and recommendations that had led her to the decision to fly her sister halfway across the country for experimental treatment, she'd watched Cait drift away further and further. Losing even the energy to smile, or whisper more than a few words.

Days, hours, minutes were precious right now. And they were slipping uncaringly between her fingers like the finest of sands.

Her spine stiffened suddenly, and she turned around to march back into the main cabin. There was a pilot who had a lot of explaining to do, and she was going to get her answers the instant he came back inside.

She might not be able to change the situation, but she was sure as hell going to understand it and all that they were up against. She didn't function well in the dark and she refused to be kept there.

Chase and Yuma returned to the plane after a mere thirty minutes. Long enough to assess their situation outside, long enough to dig through the snow at the forest's edge to find some wood and pine needles. They'd even dug a place near the plane to build a fire safely, although that was going to be difficult in this wind.

But Chase had candles onboard, and chafing dishes for those fancy flights where people expected exquisite meals. Plenty of candles. He could heat some soup, maybe even brew some coffee, but open flames in the plane made him uneasy, and they'd suck up the oxygen.

He was holding an internal debate as he and Yuma closed the door behind them. And the first words he heard were:

"Why the hell did this plane crash?"

He turned slowly, his cheeks stinging from the cold

outside. He stared at the Campbell woman, reminding himself that she was undoubtedly edgy because of her sister. And, yes, because of the crash. Plenty of reason to be truculent.

He pulled off his leather gloves while staring at her, and threw his hood back. "Well," he said slowly, "that's the question, isn't it? We ran out of fuel. Unexpectedly, inexplicably. All of a sudden. And since I had the plane in Seattle for an overhaul, I'm going to guess that somebody screwed up. But once that fuel started draining like Niagara Falls, there wasn't much I could do except try to get us down in one piece."

He waited, expecting to get his butt chewed about something, but amazingly, it didn't happen. Then she nodded. "Okay. What now? What are our chances?"

He unzipped his jacket and shrugged it off, tossing it over a seat back. "The charts I looked at before takeoff suggest the storm might last two days. That was then. It wasn't supposed to catch up to us as fast as it did. That's now. It's a helluva blow, and we aren't going to stir from the safety of this plane until it lets up."

"Two days," she said, and sounded almost frightened.

"Two days," he repeated. "If the emergency beacon is working, rescue should come soon after."

"If?"

"We didn't exactly make a soft landing. The body of the plane is twisted pretty badly. I don't know how many electrical connections are out, or what hidden damage we have. Just after we crashed, it looked like my sat-nav went out. GPS to you. And the emergency beacon needs that to tell rescuers where we are, after the storm passes. The standard transponder, which I also have, broadcasts from the underside of the plane, so we can pretty much count that out. Regardless, the storm itself will probably interfere with all radio communications, so I can't say for sure whether the problem is the weather or something is broken. I'm going to check on that right now, if you don't mind."

No objection emanated from the beauty, although her expression suggested that she'd have loved nothing better than a fight. Of course. To work off the adrenaline, probably. Or maybe she just hated the sight of him. He didn't care either way. He started to turn but her voice caught him.

"Won't they know where we are from the flight plan? From our last recorded position?"

He faced her again. "We were traveling at over six hundred miles per hour. From the time things started to go wrong, we traveled a long way. And we didn't exactly stay on the flight path while I tried to get us down on some open ground rather than in the forest. So they're going to have to search quite a wide area."

"Then you'd better make sure that beacon is working."

Chase ground his teeth. Now he was absolutely certain he didn't like her. "That thought has occurred to me as well, ma'am."

Stiff now, he turned toward the cockpit. When he got there, he closed the accordion door behind him. *This,* he thought, was not going to make anything any easier.

Rory watched the pilot close the door behind him. What was his name again? She'd paid scant attention... Oh, yeah, something like Hunter. No, Chase. Chase Dakota. He was a large enough man, well-built, with ruggedly chiseled features that hinted just a bit at a possible Native American heritage somewhere in his family tree. Gray eyes that reminded her of steel.

And not especially friendly. Although she supposed she wasn't exactly inviting friendliness at the moment. But why should she? Her sister's life was hanging in the balance, and whether this crash was his fault hardly seemed to matter. Bottom line: They had crashed and they were stuck for two days. At least two days. She would have given her right hand for some assurance that was all it would be.

She realized that Wendy had risen and was moving around toward the rear of the plane, in an alcove just behind the passenger seating but forward of the bedroom in the tail. Rory took a few steps to look and saw the redhead opening lockers above a microwave. The plane's small galley.

Needing to do something, Rory joined her.

"I'm looking at our supply situation," Wendy said, smiling. "Chase always stocks well, but it would sure be nice if I could manage to make us all something hot to drink. Soup, tea, maybe coffee."

"We can't cook. Not without a fire."

"Ah, but we might be able to manage something with candles and these chafing dishes."

"True." Rory allowed herself to be distracted by one of her favorite things: problem solving. She took a quick look at her sister and found Cait still sleeping, and gently breathing. Did parents hover over new babies like this, she wondered, waiting for the gentle rise of a chest to indicate that life continued?

She gave herself a little shake and turned back to help Wendy in the galley. "Coffee might be beyond reach," she said. "How many candles does it take to boil a pot?"

"Darned if I know. But I want my coffee, and there's a whole lot of candles. Besides, we only need to make one pot. I think the guys will build a fire outside soon. We're going to need it."

"That's for sure."

"And I'm sure if we're patient, we can heat a pot of this dried soup." She turned on the faucet and, wonder of wonders, water came out.

"Must be a gravity tank," Rory said.

"Whatever it is, it's a plus. Better to have water right now than have to melt snow on top of everything else."

While Rory worked with chafing-dish holders to elevate them enough to put fat, squat candles beneath them, bending legs and stacking a few of them, Wendy found the pieces of the drip coffeemaker and assembled them, then put coffee in the filter. "First pot of boiling water goes for coffee," she said firmly. "I need a hot drink and some caffeine."

"If you watch it, it'll never boil," Rory remarked, lighting a candle beneath her assemblage. The women shared a quiet laugh at the old joke, then together balanced a chafing dish full of water on the structure.

"I think it'll hold," Wendy said.

"It looks like it, but this time I'm going to watch it boil anyway. Too dangerous to do otherwise."

"I agree. And maybe I should speak to Chase about this."

"Why?"

Wendy tipped her head. "Because we're burning oxygen back here, and this plane is probably pretty airtight."

Rory hadn't thought of that, but as soon as Wendy spoke, she knew she was right. Planes had air exchangers, but they probably worked on electrical power like everything else. Power they didn't have now. "Go ask. I'll babysit."

Much better to have Wendy ask. Not that Chase Dakota had spared her more than a few words, but she got the feeling he didn't much care for her. Ordinarily, she didn't turn tail in the face of men like that, but right now she was acutely aware that she wasn't the person in charge. That put her on the defensive, and for now that meant stirring up as little trouble as possible.

"Houston," she muttered under her breath, "we have a problem."

Except they weren't halfway to the moon. Although they might as well have been at the moment. She heard some noise from up front and stuck her head out of the galley. Chase and Wendy's husband were pushing the door open a crack. Just a crack. Then they disappeared in the men's compound, so aptly named a cockpit, she thought sourly, and went back to their machinations with the machinery.

No emergency beacon? She refused to believe that was possible. Weren't those damn things supposed to work no matter what? Or maybe that was the cockpit race recorder she was thinking of. All of a sudden she wished she knew more about planes and less about finding and drilling for oil. Or more about cancer and her sister's condition.

She was so used to being on top of things that it killed her to consider all the things she didn't know anything about—like planes and cancer and how long it would take that damn water to boil. Because she sure would like a cup of that coffee.

Wendy rejoined her. "We might get a little chilly. They tried to open the door to a minimum so we don't suffocate, but…" She shrugged. "Nobody said camping in a blizzard in a crashed plane was going to be easy."

"What do you know about the pilot?" Rory asked. "I mean…"

Wendy's face gentled. "It's okay. He's a stranger to you and here we are in a mess. But, trust me, Chase was a military pilot before he started his charter service. He knows what he's doing, and if we lost fuel, then he's right about why. He's not the kind of guy who would authorize any maintenance shortcuts. And, as for right now, I can tell you the military gave both him and my husband a lot of survival training."

"Okay."

Something in Wendy's face changed. "Billy Joe—oh, he'd kill me if he heard me call him that to someone else—"

"Why?"

"He's just never liked his given name. He prefers everyone to call him Yuma."

"I can do that."

Wendy smiled. "I'm sure you can."

"You were going to say?"

"Yuma lived up here in these mountains for a few years after he got back from the war. Post-traumatic stress. He knows how to survive these mountains in the winter."

"That's good to know. That he's experienced, I mean, not the other."

"I understood."

"How did you two meet? Were you just neighbors?"

Wendy smiled again. "Oh, it's a much more interesting story than that. Billy Joe was a medevac pilot in Vietnam. The experience left him with a lot of nightmares, so for years he lived up in these mountains with some other vets. They just couldn't handle the bustling world at times. So they kind of built their own hermitage."

Rory nodded. "That must have been rough."

"Oh, it was. Anyway, my dad was a Vietnam vet, too, and when Billy Joe got well enough to try to return to life, Dad got him hired as our medevac pilot. Our first one, actually."

"That was nice of your dad."

"He lived to regret it." Wendy laughed quietly, letting Rory know it wasn't a bad thing. "Anyway, I had a crush on Yuma from the time I was sixteen. He was so much older and so aware of his flaws that he ran from me like a scared rabbit. And finally my dad told me to stop torturing the man."

"Ouch. That must have hurt."

"It did at first. But, you know, it finally got through my thick head that my dad was right. I was too young, too inexperienced, and Billy Joe had every reason to avoid me, and not just because I was a kid."

"So what happened?"

"I went off to nursing school, then worked in a big-city hospital for a few years until I practically had my own PTSD. When I came back here it was to become the flight nurse with the Emergency Response Team." She gave a little laugh. "You could say I wasn't exactly welcome on that helicopter."

"But something must have changed."

Wendy nodded, her gaze becoming faraway for a few minutes. "It was rough, but here we are now...together forever as Yuma likes to tease me." She turned a bit. "Is that water heating?"

Rory looked back. "I see a bit of steam on the surface."

"Good, we'll make it yet."

Even the little bit that Wendy had told her had given her an inkling of what her husband had suffered. And some of it, at least, had to be replaying in her heart and mind.

Rory sighed, realizing she wasn't the only person on this plane who had serious concerns. Yes, Cait's life hung in the balance, but surely Wendy must be worrying about Yuma and whether this would affect him.

Yet Wendy soldiered cheerfully on, confident that things would work out. Rory found herself wondering, for the first time, when she had started to lose hope for Cait. Because that's what was going on here: the loss of hope.

Not just the threat of being stranded, but the loss of hope. Did she really think nothing could save Cait now?

The thought appalled her. She shook it away, mentally stomped it into some dark place she couldn't afford to look at. Not now.

Twenty minutes later the four of them were sitting in the passenger lounge savoring hot cups of coffee. Cait still slept, but Wendy and Rory had agreed that their next task would be making soup for her.

"The way I see it," Chase said, "we need to get a fire going outside for at least a little while. We can't keep that door open too long or we'll freeze. And cooking with candles is not only slow but could be deadly."

Rory nodded agreement. No argument with him on that score.

"The wind is a beast, though, so it won't be easy. We'll need to cook, and cook fast before the fire gets buried in snow."

Rory glanced toward one of the few windows still

not covered by snow, and could see nothing but white. "It's that bad?"

"Oh, yeah," he answered her. "I don't want to burn any more candles than we absolutely must because of fire danger, but we're going to have to burn some, obviously. We've got protection against the wind, our body heat will help in a space this small, but it's still going to get pretty cold."

Rory couldn't help but glance back at the tiny bedroom where her sister slept. "I hope she can handle it."

"She's my top priority," Chase said flatly. "Cancer?"

Rory nodded. "Non-Hodgkins lymphoma. NHL for short. She hasn't got a lot of reserves left."

"I can see that. We'll keep her warm and fed if I have to light a fire in the aisle, okay?"

"I'm not sure going that far would help anyone." But for the first time she met his gaze, truly met it, and felt a pleasant, astonishing shock. It wasn't because those gunmetal eyes for the first time looked gentle, though. No, it was something else, something that heated places she was ashamed to even be aware of at such a time.

A sexual reaction at a time like this? She almost wanted to hang her head until a quiet voice in the back of her mind reminded her that adrenaline, shock and danger did funny things to a person. Life asserted itself in the most primitive way imaginable.

Plus, she was dependent on this guy. It was probably a cavewoman response, nothing more. At the same time, it felt good, shocking though it was, so she just let it be. Something in her life needed to feel good.

But it also put her on guard. She couldn't afford to lose her mental footing now—most especially now—and not to a primitive impulse to forget all sense and escape into a few moments of hot pleasure.

"What do you do?" Chase's question shocked her out of her internal dissection.

"What? Why?"

"I'm just wondering if you bring any additional skills to the table here. Yuma and I are trained in survival, and he's a huge advantage for us in that he lived in these mountains during weather like this, without so much as a cabin. Wendy's a nurse and can help take care of your sister. So what do you do?"

For the first time in her life, Rory was embarrassed to admit the truth. "I'm a petroleum geologist. I know about finding oil, and I know about drilling for it. The closest I've ever come to survival conditions was when I told the men working for me to stop drilling because they were going to hit a pocket of natural gas, and they didn't listen. And it wasn't my survival that was at stake."

Chase nodded, but didn't look scornful. Instead, all he said was, "You probably know more than you think."

"Well, I do know the air is getting stale in here and apparently you have to open the door to let in fresh, and that cools us down, too."

He nodded. "We're in a fairly airtight tube. That has advantages and disadvantages, obviously. Something I need to work on."

"And the beacon?"

"Something else I need to work on. But that's not all, Ms. Campbell."

"Call me Rory, please." Formality felt utterly awkward right now.

"I'm Chase then. Anyway, an emergency beacon works great when someone's looking for it. Assuming, of course, it's one of the things on this plane that's still working, and little enough is."

Rory felt her chest tighten with anger and something approaching despair. She had only one goal right now: get Cait into that trial before it was too late. So, of course, everything possible had gone wrong. Listening to Chase, it was hard to remember they were lucky the plane had come down reasonably intact and that no one was injured. Or maybe not just lucky. Maybe she needed to acknowledge this man's piloting expertise. But she wasn't ready to do that. Not with every new bit of information hitting her like a body blow.

Chase continued, his tone quietly emphatic, as if he were determined to make her understand. "Nobody's looking for us right now because of the storm, and we've got an additional complication…we're down in the mountains. That limits range. I don't have a satellite downlink, either, maybe because of the storm, but GPS is down, so that means the beacon can't transmit our location. And with every minute we're getting buried deeper in snow. I doubt the trail left by our slide along the mountain is going to be visible for long, if it even still is."

Her heart knocked uncomfortably. "So we're invisible."

"Right now, yes, and we're also inaccessible, so we need to conserve everything we can. After the storm passes, we might get satellite back, but I'm not going to keep trying until after the storm because I need to preserve what batteries I've got. I'll work on checking the beacon. With any luck it's still working and will work for days."

"And after the storm?" she asked. "I can't just sit here waiting indefinitely for rescue. My sister…my sister only has four days of medicine."

His answer was quiet. "I understand. Believe me.

I understand." Then he dropped another bomb. "I'm going to have to turn off the emergency lighting. That's running on batteries, too."

It was already dark in the plane. And now it was going to get even darker. Rory suppressed a shudder and tried to find the steel will that had helped her rise in what was most definitely a man's world.

Right now, however, it had deserted her. All she could do was look toward the back of the plane and her sick, dying sister, and wonder if she was going to fail Cait.

All because she'd tried to spare Cait a fatiguing, uncomfortable commercial flight. All because she'd wanted to get Cait to the hospital the fastest way possible.

Maybe sometimes fate just wouldn't let you take charge.

Chase watched the expressions play over Rory's face as she absorbed the bad news. It took real effort to read her, as if she practiced keeping a straight face, but her guard seemed to be down at the moment. She truly worried about her sister, of that he had no doubt, and her acceptance of his risk assessments suggested that she wasn't one who argued for the sake of argument. Once she had accepted that someone knew what he was doing, she didn't waste energy fighting it.

That made her fairly unique in his experience. But no less troublesome, because she really was a rare beauty, though she did nothing to enhance her looks. Not even a smidgeon of makeup highlighted her eyes, lips or cheeks. Nor did she need them. And those bright blue eyes of hers appealed to him at a deeper level than thought. A level he told himself he couldn't afford to pay attention to right now. Rescuing passengers and indulging in passions couldn't possibly mix well. Besides, as he ought to know by now, women didn't seem to like him for very long.

He shook himself free of reverie and looked at Yuma. "You said something about the wind when we were outside."

"Yeah," Yuma said. "We need to get ready to build that fire. The wind won't entirely stop, but it *will* change direction after sunset. It always does in these mountains, even in a storm. I don't know why that is, but it'll get calmer for a while and we need to be ready to take advantage of it. Ideally, we should try to make a firebox with metal, if we can find enough in here."

"We can," Chase said firmly. "The galley doors are aluminum. And there are other things, too."

"Good. Let me get one more cup of that coffee before we go out again. Damn, I'd forgotten how cold this mountain can get."

Chase saw Wendy lay her hand on Yuma's forearm, and thought again about how hard this could turn out to be for the man. Not just the plane crash, but all the resurrected memories of his time in these mountains, hiding from the demons of war that wouldn't leave him alone.

The only solution for any of them right now was to keep busy, to feel that they were accomplishing something. First rule: Leave no room for despair. Paralysis would accomplish nothing, and despair could be a killer.

"Okay," he said briskly. "Let's see about making that firebox. A hot meal would do us all some good."

He noted that Rory went first to check on her sister.

Understandable. Unfortunately, the fact that she looked more worried when she emerged concerned him.

"Is she too cold?" he asked.

"I don't think so. It's just that she's sleeping so much. Too much."

"We need to get some calories into her," he said. "Can she hold down food?"

"Mostly liquids."

"Then we'll get her some soup first thing." With that he picked up a screwdriver and started helping Yuma pull down the galley doors.

"What can I do?" Rory asked.

Chase's instinctive response was to tell her to keep an eye on her sister. Then he realized that she needed something far less passive to do. Something that made her feel like she was doing more than holding a death watch.

"There are some aluminum doors up front, too. They're faced with wood veneer, but they're aluminum. There's another screwdriver in the service hatch I left open." He wasn't sure she'd be able to work the screws—they'd been mechanically tightened—but she might surprise him. He and Yuma weren't exactly finding it impossible to loosen the screws in the galley doors.

She didn't say a word as she eased past him, but as his gaze followed her briefly, he could see a sense of purpose in her posture and step. Good.

Then he watched Wendy slip back into the bedroom to check on their patient. Rory, he suspected, hadn't wanted to let anyone else touch her sister. A born guard dog. He liked that.

Chase and Yuma carried the aluminum doors outside into the blizzard to hammer them into the shape they needed. Neither of them wanted to do it in the confines of the plane because the banging would be deafening.

Ignoring the cold and the snow that stung like small knives, they battered the doors into a box with a top. Removing a couple of the inset latches created for air to circulate.

"Instant stove," Chase remarked an hour later.

"Hardly instant," Yuma replied. "I'm soaked with sweat."

"That'll teach you to wear warm clothes in the dead of winter."

Yuma chuckled. "Better than being out here in rags with ratty blankets."

"Guess so." Chase paused after shaking the firebox to ensure it was sturdy. "You doing okay?"

"I'm fine. Yeah, I'm remembering, but the memories of being out here aren't memories of Nam. It's too damn cold."

Chase laughed. "I guess I can see that."

Yuma stood straight and looked toward the almost invisible trees that surrounded the clearing. "Can I be honest, Chase?"

"Hell, yeah." But Chase felt himself tightening inwardly, ready for criticism he felt he deserved.

"You did an amazing job of bringing us down. I'm not sure how you managed it. We're alive because of it."

Chase waited, sure there was more, but it didn't come immediately. Finally, Yuma sighed, the sound almost snatched away by the wind.

"I'm grateful," he said. "More grateful than I can tell you because honest to God, Chase, I'm not sure I could survive without Wendy."

Chase felt his chest tighten in sympathy, but didn't know what to say.

"Do you know I used to be an alcoholic?"

"I was probably too young to hear that rumor."

Yuma chuckled and looked at him. "Yeah, probably. But I was. It was a way to hide. Anyway, I got my act cleaned up before Wendy came back to town to take her second swing at my bachelorhood. Thing was, even then I kept a bottle in my desk drawer."

"I thought you weren't supposed to do that."

"I wasn't." Yuma's mouth tightened a bit. "It was my security blanket. I knew it was right there if I ever couldn't fight off the urge for a drink. For me, anyway, it kept the craving from going over the top."

"I never would have thought that of you."

Yuma shrugged. "It wouldn't work for most folks, I guess, but it worked for me. Never even broke the seal on the bottle. And then Wendy…well, I haven't needed to keep a bottle around since."

Chase nodded, getting the message. Or at least he thought he did. "You've got a lot to be proud of."

"Actually, no, I don't," Yuma said flatly. "Pride doesn't figure into it at all. What I have is a lot to be grateful for, like that woman in there." He paused. "We gotta save Rory's sister, man."

"I know."

"I know you do." Yuma took a step toward the trees. "That's why I respect you. Now let's got get some wood and some pine needles."

Two hours later they had the firebox assembled and working outside. From the window of the plane, Rory watched as the fire burned within the three-sided box.

It had taken some effort to make a chimney so it would draw air up and through, but it was working now.

Dimly in the swirling snow, she could see the men looking for more wood to keep it going. It was getting darker out there now, as night closed in on them.

She ordinarily liked the night, but not this time. The plane had gone dark to save battery power. The only light came from a lone candle sitting on the large work or dining table in the center of four of the seats.

As business jets went, this was a comfortably sized one, capable of carrying twelve or more passengers, with room to move around. She wondered what kind of traffic Chase could carry to pay for a plane like this, then let the thought wander off. What did it matter? There were apparently enough people left in the world who could afford this kind of transportation, and given that it was a plane, being based out of some invisible town in Wyoming was hardly a hindrance to him.

Reluctantly, she tore her gaze from the fire, experiencing a gut-deep understanding of why fire had been so important in times past. Probably since ancient times. It promised life, light, warmth. It held the night at bay.

Nothing inside this plane did that except for a single candle.

It was time to wake Cait and get her to take her medicine. Rory had hoped to feed her soup at the same time, but she couldn't wait any longer. Wendy had heated enough water to make a couple of cups of tea, but no more because they had to be careful.

"Lots of sugar in it," she said to Rory now as she passed her a mug. "And there's another if she wants it."

"Thanks."

She accepted the mug, testing the temperature of the tea with her upper lip. Not hot enough to burn. Good.

Then she grabbed the small nylon bag in which she kept Cait's meds, and headed back, aware that Wendy followed with the candle. A candle in the dark.

Cripes. She needed more than that.

Once in the bedroom, Wendy set the candle on the small bedside table, then slipped away to leave the sisters alone.

"Cait. Cait?" Gently she shook her sister's shoulder. "Cait?"

Slowly, Cait's eyes opened, and she sighed. "Why don't you just let me go?"

Rory's heart stuttered. "Because I can't. Not until we've tried everything."

Cait's eyes fluttered. "I guess."

"Cait, just because Hal left you doesn't mean there's nothing left to live for. You don't need me to tell you that. Now I've got a fresh cup of sweet tea for you."

"And medicine. Always medicine."

"Yeah, medicine. I'm glad I have it. Do you think I can help you sit up a bit?"

"Sure." Cait sounded utterly listless. Rory didn't let that stop her. She lifted her sister carefully, propping her up on pillows.

"Try some tea first," she suggested. "It'll give you energy."

Holding the cup to her sister's lips, she got half of it down her, tiny sip by tiny sip. And as the sugar hit her system, Cait seemed to gain a little energy. Just a little.

Then came the pills. This part sucked, because Cait wasn't finding it all that easy to swallow anymore, not since the radiation treatments. But they got those down, too.

"Great," Rory said, with a smile she didn't feel. Talk about a small handful of pills being an ordeal. "There's another cup of tea for you. I'll go get it."

"I already have."

Rory turned to see Wendy standing in the doorway with another mug in hand.

"Hi, Cait, I'm Wendy."

Cait gave a little nod. "So there are other passengers on the plane?"

"Me and my husband," Wendy said, moving forward to exchange mugs with Rory. "When you get a little more rested, you'll have to join us in the cabin. I'll bet we've all got interesting stories to trade."

Rory expected Cait to decline, but instead was astonished to see her sister smile, however weakly. "Sounds like fun."

"It will be. All of us have had some crazy experiences. I'll bet Rory has had more than her share. And you can keep her honest for us." Wendy winked and slipped out again.

"I like her," Cait whispered.

"Me, too. More tea?"

The second cup went down easier than the first. Unfortunately, almost as soon as it was gone, Cait's eyes fluttered closed and she slipped away again. A few words and a couple of cups of tea had been enough to wear her out.

That was not good, not good at all. Rory had the awful feeling that she could almost see the darkness gathering around her sister, waiting to claim her.

No. God, no. She jumped up, forcing the vision away. She couldn't afford to let such thoughts even cross her mind.

You're not getting her, she thought between anger and despair. *You're not taking my sister away!*

The silence seemed to mock her.

Chapter 3

Dinner worked out quite well, given the arduous conditions outside. At least they weren't going to starve, Rory thought. Cait even managed to swallow a cup of soup and another cup of heavily sweetened tea. This time she asked to join them in the cabin.

Rory's heart swelled almost to breaking. As soon as she bent to lift her sister, Chase appeared and did it for her.

"Nice you can join us, little lady," he said as he carried her, wrapped in her blankets, to one of the chairs near the table. "You get too tired, just let me know, okay? And if you want, the seats recline all the way so you can lie down out here."

"Thanks," Cait managed.

Rory could only look at Chase with gratitude. He had stepped in at the right moment and said exactly the right thing. Not too much, not too little.

And Cait looked content for the first time since Rory had come home to learn how sick she was. These plane seats were wider than normal and deeply padded, so Cait seemed to have no difficulty curling up in a way that made her feel comfortable. She didn't say much, and occasionally she seemed to doze, but she also paid more attention than usual to the conversation around her. She even accepted another cup of tea, and this time held it herself.

There was hope, Rory thought. There was definitely hope. She glanced toward Chase and saw the same expression in his eyes that she was feeling. He, too, seemed to see something promising in Cait's effort.

But the wind and the cold soon reminded them that this was no social occasion. The plane groaned loudly again as a particularly strong gust buffeted it, but nothing moved. They'd be buried by morning, Rory thought. Completely and totally buried in snow. Then what? Panic fluttered through her in a single quick wave.

"Let's get down more blankets," Chase said. "Then I think we should bundle in for the night. I'll take first watch."

"Watch?" Rory asked.

He nodded. "We're going to burn at least one candle all night—more if necessary. Someone has to keep an eye on it. We also need to watch the cabin temperature so we don't turn into popsicles overnight."

Cait had dozed off again. "She'll be warmer here, won't she?"

"Probably," he answered. "As long as she's comfortable, I'd leave her."

"I'll keep an eye on her," Wendy said. "Yuma and I are just going to curl up together on these seats right behind her. Why don't you take the chance to stretch out in the back for a bit?"

"I don't feel sleepy," Rory admitted. Not in the least. Her mind wouldn't stop racing; she had too many worries.

"Fine," Chase said. "You can come up front and keep first watch with me. Make sure *I* don't fall asleep."

She almost offered to stand watch in his stead, but caught herself just in time. He was the captain of this plane, after all, and she suspected that meant pretty much the same thing in the air as at sea. And while she didn't defer to men simply because they were men, she *did* defer to rank unless given good reason not to. There was just no point in stepping on some toes.

"Thanks, I think I will."

Maybe it would ease the terror at the back of her mind, the terror that they wouldn't be found in time to save Cait. She'd seemed better for a while, but Rory knew how illusory that could be.

They settled in the two cockpit chairs with the accordion door closed behind them. There was no light at all, except one small red one.

"What's that?" she asked.

"Control for the emergency lights. I can operate them manually when I need to. Thank goodness."

Thank goodness indeed. She suspected that if all those cabin lights had been left burning, the ones that guided the way to the emergency exits, they'd have gone dark for good by now. "Everything else is down?"

"For now. No point wasting any resources yet."

"I suppose not." Then, "So you really think a fuel line broke or something?"

"Or something," he agreed. In the dark, he kept his voice quiet. "We have wing tanks, but there's a central compartment where the fuel meets and mixes so that the tanks can be balanced. Make sense?"

"Yes."

"We could get in trouble if one tank or the other got used up too fast. We'd not only be struggling to balance ourselves, but we might lose an engine. So everything meets in the middle and fuel is passed back and forth. Considering that we lost fuel from both tanks simulta-neously and rapidly, I figure something went wrong in the central holding tank. And at the rate we were losing fuel, I suspect it was being pumped out of the plane."

"There's a mechanism for that, right, to empty the fuel?"

"Yes. We can dump fuel for an emergency landing."

"So that might have gotten screwed up?"

"Maybe. Something sure as hell did, and we won't know until the NTSB takes a look. I know I got no cockpit warning of any kind until the fuel started to get too low. I'd already noticed the gauges were falling too fast, but no indication as to *why*."

"And there should have been?"

"The way these babies are designed, this plane shouldn't hiccup without giving me some kind of alert. What's more, once I noticed the fuel dropping, we were over the mountains, airports behind us were closed and I still thought for a while I'd have enough. I never cut it that close, despite the weight of excess fuel."

"So maybe two things went wrong."

"So it would seem. But it did happen awfully fast. I'm just glad I was able to get us down in one piece. For a while there, I didn't think I was going to."

"I'm glad you did, too."

She heard him shift, and as her eyes adapted to the

near absence of light, except for the tiny bit of red from dash, she could see that he looked her way as he spoke.

"Look, I'm worried about your sister, too. Seriously worried. But if we had to crash in a blizzard, having an intact plane is about as cozy as it could possibly be."

"I guess. Right now it feels like a damn prison."

"That, too." He didn't argue with her, and for a moment she felt a bit embarrassed by her ingratitude. But then she let it go. Right now this plane *was* a prison as much as it was a shelter.

"So what exactly do you do?" he asked her.

"I own a consulting firm. We prospect for oil, and supervise initial drilling to ensure that our clients locate the well optimally. Most of my work these days is in Mexico."

"Do you enjoy it?"

"It's like a great big treasure hunt, in one way. In another it's a pain."

"Why?"

"Because it's a man's world, why else? More so south of the border."

He was silent for a minute. It was a silence so intense she could hear their breathing. Apparently, between the soundproofing of the plane and the mounding snow, nothing else could penetrate this cocoon.

"That would be rough," he said finally. "I watched plenty of women pilots face that stuff in the military. At least they had regulations on their side. You wouldn't."

"And a whole culture against me. Well, not entirely, but you know how that goes. At one job, I had a *curandera* come out and promise to place a curse on anyone who gave me a hard time. It was a last resort, but it worked."

"Can you work anywhere else?"

"Most of the oil in the world seems to be in the wrong places for women to go."

"But you get hired anyway?"

"I'm good at what I do. It may be a boy's game, but I play it with the best. So I charge enough to pay some bodyguards, and sometimes to get a *bruja,* a witch, on my side."

"Sounds almost like being in a war zone."

"Sometimes. It's not the pros who give me trouble, it's the local hires. Usually they settle down with time. They know where the pay is coming from."

"But what about that blowout you mentioned?"

"Ah, that. Well, a couple of guys with more machismo than sense didn't listen when I told them our seismograph readings indicated that we were about to hit a pocket of natural gas. You always hit some gas, and there are precautions to take. I mean, depending on the depth, that stuff explodes out of the well under some huge pressure and a single spark is enough to cause a conflagration. We weren't ready to open the gas pocket, I told them to wait, but they had some kind of incentive or bet on the line and ignored me. I'm just glad I got everybody else out of the area. Then, of course, we had a messed-up rig and a roman candle to put out."

"And the guys?"

"They lived. Nice burns, though. I don't think they'll ignore orders again."

She saw him shake his head, though she couldn't read his expression. "You live an exciting life."

"Sometimes. Ah, I mostly like the people I meet down there. I love the little towns, the pace of life, the color, the music. Roughnecks are just a tough group anywhere. When I'm viewed as a tourist I have a great time. The problem starts when I'm the boss."

"I guess I can see that."

"And it would happen just about anywhere. It's like anything—you take the good with the bad. So you were a military pilot?"

"Yeah. I flew off carriers."

She leaned back a little and twisted, trying to see him better. "I read a story about that once. A true story."

"What's that?"

"It was in Korea, I think. Some navy and air-force pilots were arguing about whether the navy pilots had a tougher landing to make, and the air-force pilots claimed they could land on a carrier no problem."

At that a snort escaped him. "Why do I know how this is going to end?"

"Probably because you've landed on carriers. I guess they went out and drew the outline of a carrier deck and took turns landing. Needless to say…"

"I can imagine. And the navy guys probably crowed that the deck wasn't even moving."

"I believe that was part of it."

"There's a part they probably left out, though."

"Which is?"

"The tailhook."

Rory wouldn't have believed it was possible, but she laughed out loud. "You're right. I don't think that was mentioned."

"Of course not," he said drily. "Look, I won't tell you it's easier landing on a moving deck, but with the navigational aides we've got and the tailhook, it's not as hard as trying to land in that amount of space on flat ground *without* a tailhook."

"I don't need a map to get that one." She hesitated, then asked, "Why'd you leave? You seem too young to have retired."

"I failed my flight physical. And before you get all upset because I'm still a pilot, let me explain. Flight physicals in the military are rigorous beyond belief. Most guys will fail before they reach thirty-five. So some little glitch shows up, one that won't keep you from flying, won't prevent you from getting a job with a commercial airline, but it *will* prevent you from flying combat missions or doing carrier landings. Those are the rules. We're still allowed to fly, to keep our flight status, but we're off the books for actual missions."

"That seems extreme."

"Probably not. We *do* pull a lot of high Gs. Anyway, once I couldn't make carrier landings anymore, I didn't want a desk job so I resigned."

"And built your own little airline."

"One plane and me, a long way from my own airline, but basically, yeah."

"And now your livelihood is lying buried in snow on the side of a mountain."

"So it is." His voice sounded tight, but then he let out a breath. "The important thing is getting everyone out alive. Then I'll deal with the NTSB, the company that did the overhaul and my insurance carrier. By the time all that's taken care of, I would almost bet I'll be ready to kill someone."

"You'll certainly be older."

A quiet laugh escaped him. "Goes without saying."

Concern for her sister, which had been eating her alive for weeks now, cracked open just a little, allowing her to feel for him. "I'm sorry. I know how miserable that crap can be. I went through it on the blowout. I don't know what was worse—dealing with the investigators or dealing with the insurers."

"They were probably both equally bad. They have

the same goal after all—to give somebody *else* a hard time."

Another chuckle escaped her. "Oh, yeah. And to pin blame, preferably somewhere that doesn't cause *them* any problems."

"So what did they decide on that blowout?"

"I feared it was going to be pinned on me as long as the roughnecks stuck together. Easier to blame the *gringa* than the guys you have to work with. I was more than a little surprised to find out that a certain amount of gratitude made them tell the truth, how I had ordered the drilling stopped, and then, when I was disobeyed, cleared the area. At least nobody tried to say I should have halted the drilling myself."

"Could you have?"

"Short of shooting two men, no. And by the time I got back to the site, it was too late. I'd ordered the drilling stopped that morning, then I had to run over to another site where they were complaining that the hole was dry, and by the time I got back…well, we were minutes from disaster. All I could do was tell everyone to clear out."

She paused to sigh. "Oil wells stink when they're pumping oil. Gas is mixed in, of course, but the hydrogen sulfide smell—rotten eggs—is enough to make you gag. There was no smell. They drilled into a pocket of pure methane, and it was odorless. That is so freaking rare. I had no idea they had already broken through when I started shouting for everyone to get away, and screamed again for those guys to stop the drill. No idea. I expected the smell. Maybe they did, too. I don't know."

"So the gas was everywhere?"

"Damn near. It couldn't have been long, though.

Methane is heavier than air. It sinks to ground level. If enough of it had been out there, people would have started getting asphyxiated, and the flash fire would have singed everything at ground level. Instead, we just blew the well."

She twisted toward him. "That's why we have to burn off the escaping gas if we can't manage to capture it. Because it sinks, and when it sinks it's deadly. In the case of that well, we may have been saved by a good breeze. I don't know. I'll never know. I wasn't there when they initially busted into the pocket so I have no idea how much gas just dissipated on the wind or how little escaped right before the explosion."

"But why would those guys press on against orders?"

"Because I'm not the only boss. I'm the geologist. I find the oil, I try to keep them on track until they get the field open. There are other bosses, there isn't anything like unions for those workers, people get paid crap, and if the guy running the drilling operation, say, is getting paid by the well, and not by the hour, he'd have a lot of incentive not to want things to slow down. And he might create incentives for his crews to push on, regardless of safety. I don't know. I really, truly don't know. I know what they want me to know, and I know what I can figure out from my explorations. Beyond that…" she shrugged. "The actual business end of what's happening is opaque to me. I hear rumors, sometimes, but that's it."

"Sounds like a dangerous situation to be in."

"Not usually. Most drillers are cautious and good at what they do. Most of the people working these jobs want to bring in a sound well, not a rocket. We have more problems from faulty equipment than from greedy people. For all I know, the entire thing may have happened because someone didn't want to take orders from a woman."

"Will you be going back when your sister recovers?"

She appreciated the way he posed that question. Her chest tightened a bit, but she squelched the feeling. She'd been alone for a long time, and she could handle this situation on her own. She couldn't afford to show weakness because a stranger was being kind. "I'm not sure," she said finally. "We'll have to see how it goes."

She heard his seat creak as he shifted. "I'm going back to check on the candle, make sure everyone's okay."

"I'll go with you." She couldn't stand the thought of sitting here alone in the dark with that one red, unblinking eye. And checking on Cait had become an absolute compulsion for her.

"How come you have so many candles?" she asked him just before he opened the door.

"I've got even more in my hangar. An errant order got me a lifetime's supply, and the restocking fee was huge beyond belief."

That brought a smile to her lips and lifted her spirits a bit. It seemed that life happened to everyone.

"They make great gifts," he said quietly, a note of humor in his voice. "Well, they did until people started running when they saw me coming."

Everything in the cabin seemed fine. Rory bent over her sister, touching her cheeks, finding them cool but not too cool. She waited a moment, until she felt the flutter of her sister's breath. All was good for now.

The wind's buffeting made the plane creak a bit, but quietly now, not as loudly as earlier. Rory guessed that meant they were getting buried.

"I need some coffee," Chase said. "And since it's cooling down in here, we need to burn a couple of extra candles anyway."

"Oxygen?"

He pointed to the door. "I think enough can get in through that hole the lock left, but if it starts to feel at all stuffy, let me know. The candle seems to be burning normally though, which is a good sign."

Maybe the only sign they'd have, Rory thought. If the candle flames dimmed, they'd know they were in trouble. Like canaries in a coal mine. And a darned good reason to keep watches.

She stepped into the galley and by the light of a freshly lit candle reassembled the stand she'd made earlier from some of the chafing-dish holders. A couple of candles below and soon water was heating.

Rory leaned back against the bulkhead and wrapped her arms around herself. It seemed chillier back here.

"Where's your jacket?" Chase asked.

"In the overhead bin above Cait. I don't want to wake her."

He turned, slipping into the bedroom, and came back a minute later with a royal blue blanket. He draped it over her shoulders and helped tuck it around her. She appreciated the gesture. Maybe not *all* men were meatheads, she thought.

"Doesn't to let yourself get cold," he said, and rubbed her upper arms briskly. "It's harder to warm up than to stay warm."

"That's not something I've had to think about the last few years. If anything, I've spent most of my time being too warm."

In the candlelight, she caught the gleam of his smile. It was a nice smile. With that one expression he made her acutely aware that she was a woman and he was a man. And that it had been a very long time since she'd let a man get this close or touch her. She couldn't afford it on the job, or anywhere near the job, and that consumed most of her life.

It also had left her with a less-than-flattering opinion of men. Getting her a blanket, she reminded herself, didn't mean he was any better than the rest.

But then she remembered the way he had carried Cait, as if she were precious cargo, and she felt her heart lurch a bit. He could be gentle. Kind. Concerned. And so far she had to admit he seemed admirably calm and collected considering that everything he had worked for lay in ruins around him. She wouldn't have blamed him for a little display of anger or irritation or *something,* given what had happened to his plane.

Heck, after the blowout, once the injured guys had been removed and the recovery team had come in to try to extinguish the fire, she'd kicked in one of the doors in her trailer. She wasn't proud of it, but sometimes adrenaline and temper got the best of her.

She shivered unexpectedly.

"You're cold," he said.

"I can't be. I'm not any colder than anyone else."

"But you've been living in southern climes. You're going to feel it more than the rest of us."

And without so much as a by-your-leave, he unzipped his jacket, tugged the blanket open and stepped inside it with her. He urged her arms to slip around him inside his jacket, then wrapped his around her.

She sucked a sharp breath, about to protest instinctively. Then, "My God, you feel like a heater!"

"I've been nicely bundled up. And I'm willing to share."

All he did was share. Not by the merest movement did he suggest or hint at anything except that he was giving her his body heat. But he might as well have.

The full-frontal pressure of their bodies immediately unleashed a whole different kind of heat in her. She became all too acutely aware of the hardness of his chest, the flatness of his belly. He managed to keep his pelvis from touching her, so she had no idea if he felt the same response. But she knew what she wanted. She wanted him to bear down on her, make her forget by taking her right here, right now, still fully clothed. A few awkward gropings, some needy pressure…and a rocket trip to the stars would result.

She was that close, and it astonished her that such thoughts should even enter her mind. When she dated, she was a dinner-and-flowers type of woman. She always wanted a courtship, time, a slow progression while she sorted through her feelings.

So much for that. Right now a caveman would have gotten her consent. And all because having Chase Dakota lean against her to keep her warm was suddenly the sexiest damn thing in the world.

She closed her eyes as feelings of desire tormented her. Every nerve in her body seemed to have awakened, become hypersensitive. A heaviness between her legs turned into a slow throbbing, the pulsebeat of need. She heard her breathing deepen and speed up a little all at once, and hoped it didn't betray her.

Heavens, she couldn't remember ever having felt a craving this strong or elemental. It had nothing to do with the kind of person Chase was, and everything to do with the fact that she was a woman, he was a man, and her response was coming from somewhere besides her conscious mind.

Basic. Instinctual. And oh, so good. It was as if she had contained a bottled genie all her life and somehow Chase had just pulled the cork. She didn't recognize the response she was having, but she couldn't argue that it wasn't her.

It was definitely her, as well as something about the man who held her close for no other reason than to make her warm.

"Getting warm?" he asked.

She had to struggle against impulses to answer. "Yes. Thank you." A mere breath of sound.

"Good. We need to keep you wrapped up."

In his arms? Oh, yes. But of course that wasn't what he meant.

"You were colder than you realized," he said. "I felt it."

And what else had he felt, she wondered. Then to her dismay, he was pulling back from her, tucking the blanket around her. She was definitely warmer now, and his action brought her back to her senses. They were making coffee, not a safe process under these conditions, and one they couldn't afford to leave unattended, even supposing he had felt the same shaft of desire she had.

He turned, lifted the lid on the chafing dish and looked. "The water's boiling."

A few minutes later when they stepped out of the galley area with their coffee, Rory immediately noticed how much cooler the cabin was. She looked at Chase over her shoulder and he nodded.

"More candles," he said quietly. "You go sit, I'll get them."

They had made a little pocket of heat in the galley, even though it had no door on it, but stepping into the larger space gave Rory an indication of just how much the temperature was dropping in here.

Chase returned with a bunch of thick candles and set them on the tables that served the passenger seating. Soon they all glowed, driving the night out of the cabin. Rory wondered how long it would take them to drive out the cold as well.

"Now we absolutely can't afford to sleep," Rory remarked as Chase took the seat next to her.

"Nope," he agreed.

Rory watched the flames as she sipped her coffee, trying to imagine the rate at which those candles would use oxygen, and how much oxygen there was in a cabin the size of this plane. She didn't have enough information, of course, but making those mental calculations was a distraction.

Distraction from the hunger she still felt for the man sitting beside her. Even though it had been tamped, wisps remained, reminding her.

She glanced his way. "Do you always wear jeans and sweatshirts when you fly?"

A soft chuckle escaped him. "I was ferrying my plane back from Seattle. I picked up Wendy and Yuma because they were out there for a conference and I couldn't see them taking a commercial flight when I was bringing the plane back anyway. Then you showed up, wanting to go immediately. Sorry, I forgot the uniform at home. I wasn't expecting to need it."

"I was just curious. I've seen plenty of bush pilots dressed like you, but never one running a business charter."

"What I wear depends on the client. Most of them don't see much of me anyway."

"I guess not. So ordinarily you'd have a cabin attendant?"

"Usually a couple of them. People who hire jets for business expect to be treated like precious cargo. There are exceptions, of course. Some people just want to be left alone to work. Or romance each other."

Another trickle of desire warmed her between her thighs. It had been an offhand comment but, like a teenage girl, she responded to it as provocative. She wanted to shake her head at herself. "Must be interesting."

"It can be. But, again, I'm usually at the controls and hear about most of it later. Not that there's usually a lot to hear."

"So you actually are based out of Wyoming?"

"Yes."

"I guess that's not out of the way, when you fly."

"Not really. The bulk of my work is out West. I fly a lot of oil types around the Northwest, into Canada, sometimes to Alaska. Some bankers. Some ranchers, but mostly guys who own companies like yours. Only occasionally do I fly someone back East, but it happens."

"I can't imagine spending my money this way."

"Except this one time."

She looked back toward her sleeping sister. "Except this one time," she agreed. "I'm not rich. I do all right, and I'm not complaining. But I didn't get into this to get rich—I got into it because it fascinates me. It's not every job that can take you all over the world to do the thing you love."

"True."

"And it's not every job that will let you pull out all the stops to help your sister."

He nodded, his expression hard to read in the flickering light. "I kind of mucked that up."

"From what you said, it wasn't your fault."

"Maybe not. But I hired the company to do the overhaul. I picked them."

"Have they worked for you before?"

"Yeah."

"Well then."

He gave a quiet snort. "Yeah. Well then. We'll get Cait out of here as soon as the storm is over. Do you believe me?"

"I have to believe you," she said quietly. "I *have* to."

Chapter 4

The wind blew ice crystals hard against the side of the plane, and even with the soundproofing Chase could hear the *shhh* of it against the metal or windows. A mean night out there, not fit for man or beast. A killer night.

He looked at Rory. "You got enough winter clothes?"

"You mean we may have to hike out of here?"

"I don't know yet. But if we do, what have you got? Boots? Gloves?"

"Yeah. I picked up a bunch of stuff from an outfitter in Seattle. I was promised Minnesota gets pretty cold in the winter, and I figured I couldn't spend every minute at the hospital."

"Where is it?"

"In my carry-on in the overhead bin."

"Which one?"

"Why?"

He sighed. "Because I want to check it out. I want to know everything we're up against. Right here we could make it a few weeks with candles and food. But your sister can't. We may need to make some decisions."

"You want to know if I can walk out of here."

"If necessary."

She shook her head. "My sister can't."

"I know that. I'm already figuring out how to deal with that. But what I need to know is if everyone *else* can walk out of here."

At last she quit questioning him and stood up. She popped the bin open and pulled down a large carry-on. He was just glad she hadn't said it was all in the cargo space below them. First of all, he couldn't get to it, and second of all, it would probably have been flattened like a pancake if not ripped up.

Somebody had advised her well, he thought as he clicked on a flashlight to look at what she had. Water-proof boots with removable liners, great for hiking. A parka for subzero temps with a snorkel hood to protect the face, a thick pair of lined gloves, a pair of ski over-alls to protect the legs from cold and wind. Even some Thinsulate undergarments. She'd be okay.

"Good," he said, and leaned back. "I suggest you put those boots on now. You never know. Did you get extra liners for them?"

"Yes."

He nodded. "You got good advice."

"I never settle for less."

He could well believe it. And it also seemed to him that she had come totally prepared for something a lot less civilized than the Minneapolis area. But maybe that was her mind-set after so many years drilling in jungles and on mountainsides. Never cut a corner.

He was a great believer in that himself. He leaned back while she put the boots on. Then she walked quietly down the aisle, just a few feet, to check on her sister. He watched the tender way she touched Cait's cheek and adjusted the blankets around her, careful not to disturb her.

He rose and eased his way back, planning to reheat the coffee. He wasn't ready by any means to change watches yet, and coffee was his second-favorite thing in life, the first being flying.

"She okay?" he whispered before he edged past.

"Fine."

He realized that she had followed him back to the galley only when he turned to face the coffeepot assemblage.

"She seems warm enough, and her breathing is normal for her. No sign of distress."

"That's good. Very good." He lit the candle under the pot, figuring there were maybe two cups left in it. "Want some? Although you ought to think about sleeping."

"Coffee never keeps me awake," she said with a half smile. "Sometimes I wish it could. I'll go get the mugs."

He'd planned to just bring the pot forward, but instead he nodded. Better to have her gone for a minute so he could steel himself again.

Because the simple truth was, hugging her to help warm her up earlier had proved to be a huge mistake. One of epic proportions. You could get kicked to the curb just so often by women before you developed a set of rules to live by.

First rule: If it might last more than a few hours, avoid it. Second rule: Never wake up in anyone else's bed.

Well, he'd screwed up this time, because as soon as

he'd wrapped his arms around Rory, some part of him had realized that a few hours would never be enough, and that he'd probably wake up in her bed if he ever crossed the line.

He couldn't exactly put his finger on why that was, either. He knew he'd had an instantaneous sexual response to her, but that alone meant nothing. Something else had set off the klaxon in his head, and he'd had to fight to stand there holding her rather than skittering away in a quest for self-protection. At least she probably hadn't noticed. Her concern for her sister clearly occupied damn near her entire horizon.

But he had noticed. The response he'd had had remained indelibly imprinted on the most primitive part of his brain, waking every now and then to remind him that Rory was sexy. Sexier than sexy. For some reason she represented a trap, not a fling.

He sighed, leaned forward against the narrow counter and sniffed the coffee. It was just starting to heat.

Rory returned, bearing their mugs. She emptied the dregs into the sink. "How much water do we have?"

"Plenty. If not, look outside."

She pursed her lips at him. "I get that part. I'm thinking in terms of water we need to keep unfrozen. Like for the loo."

"Chemical toilet. I don't know if the collection tank is leaking, but if it is, it won't affect function, although it'll be awful for the environment. I should have enough in the supply tank to last us many, many days. The only water we need is for ourselves."

Just then the plane tipped. Not a whole lot, but Chase felt it in every fiber of his being. Then it seemed to slide, just a little.

He cussed.

"What's going on?" she asked.

"I don't know. If we're sliding, we can't go far. Maybe pressure is melting some of the snow under the plane, lubricating it."

But he wasn't going to guess. He blew out the candle under the coffee and headed forward. He paused just long enough to whisper something in Yuma's ear. Yuma's head popped up, but he didn't move a single other muscle. Wendy remained asleep beside him.

Yuma nodded, then Chase went up front and started pulling out his outer gear.

"I'm coming with you," Rory said, and started pulling on her own gear, including the insulated ski pants.

"It's probably nothing," he said.

"Probably. Then again, you might need help."

His first instinct was to tell her to stay put. But he looked at her again, remembering that she had a rather tough background in her own business. She might be resourceful in a million ways he couldn't even imagine now. So he simply let her finish dressing.

They popped the hatch open, crawled swiftly out, then closed it again.

The night might as well have been pitch. Usually in a snowstorm, the snow magnified just a little light into brightness. But there was no light tonight. Not a moon, not a star, not a streetlamp or house lights. Any candle glow was now completely concealed behind windows buried in snow.

He'd been in darkness like this before, where you couldn't even gather enough light to know where to put your foot, in places he would never name. He hated it.

Chase snapped on his flashlight and instantly the night changed. The wildly blowing snow became visible, but vision hardly got any better. What darkness had hidden before, the snow did now. But not as much.

He could see the fuselage, at least some of it, now nearly hidden beneath snow in some places, blown bare in others. Walking slowly around, scanning the wreck, he heard Rory's boots crunch right behind him. In case the plane was shifting, he took the longer route around the tail section to come up the other side. Then he saw what had happened.

He came upon the wing, and noted that it had opened a crack between the snow beneath it and the snow mounding on the wing.

"There," he said.

"What?"

"The wind must have caught the wing just right and given it some lift." He waited, playing his flashlight over it, giving her a chance to take it in.

"That's what it looks like," she agreed finally.

He glanced toward her, but could see nothing of her face in the snorkel hood.

He squatted down and pulled off his glove, picking up some snow. She squatted facing him.

"Dry," he said. "The snow is so damn dry it's not going to pack. This'll probably happen again."

"Nothing we can do?"

"Nope. Even if we shove snow around the wing, the wind is just going to carry it away again."

"Do we need to get off the plane?"

"It's not like we have anywhere to go. There are trees maybe a hundred and fifty yards in front of us, so even if we're on ice we can't slide far. And trust me, no matter how aerodynamic that wing is, it's not going to be able to carry us far on a wind like this. All it can do is shake us a bit."

"Okay."

"I want to finish looking around, though." Wanted to make sure nothing had changed that he needed to worry about. Besides, doing a visual on his aircraft was a habit so deeply ingrained he couldn't have broken it.

He half wished, however, that he could find something to deal with. Anything. He wasn't accustomed to sitting on his hands doing next to nothing in a situation like this. He needed something to sink his teeth into.

Other than dealing with the crash, the destruction of his plane and the concern about his passengers. Those were all emotional things, and right now he was pretty much putting them on hold. What he needed was some useful action, but the weather right now precluded any kind of action.

"Sure." She followed him around the wing toward the nose.

He stood there, playing the flashlight over the mounded snow that buried the nose and cockpit. It had compressed during their landing, but now he could see that it was beginning to dry and sift away. The character of the snow was changing.

"It amazes me," he said, raising his voice to be heard over the howling wind and the hissing snow, "that when we first landed that snow was packed tight. Now tell me how a storm so dry can keep making snow."

"Maybe it's not. Maybe it's blowing the same stuff over and over because it's so dry."

"Probably. Makes no practical difference, I guess. We still have to wait it out."

"Yeah." Her snorkel turned toward him, her face still concealed. "This has to be awful for you," she said. "Your plane, I mean. I know how I feel when a well blows, and it's not even my equipment."

"That's stuff I can deal with later. Right now I'm more concerned about four passengers—most especially your sister."

She remained silent and still for a beat. Then, "Thank you. She's my foremost concern."

The wind suddenly shifted, blowing crazily from one direction then another until the snow seesawed wildly in the air. "Let's get back inside. Nothing we can do out here right now."

As they crawled back into the plane, icy air snaked down the aisle and carried some snow with it. Just a sprinkling that sparkled in the candlelight. The candles themselves flickered then brightened. Chase was able to bring the door back up himself, and when he turned around, he saw Yuma coming forward with a couple of mugs in his hands.

"Figured you'd be cold," he said.

Rory was already bending over her sister, still wearing her outer gear, but she'd thrown her hood back so she could lean close and check Cait. Chase accepted the mug from Yuma without taking his eyes from her, which is why he caught the way she stiffened.

At once he set the mug on the table, squeezed past Yuma and headed back. "Rory?"

"Her breathing doesn't sound quite right. And she feels warm."

Hoping against hope that it was the contrast after being outside, he touched his own fingers to Cait's cheek. "Hell," he whispered.

Rory turned. "Wendy? Wendy?"

Wendy's eyes fluttered open. An instant later she was fully awake. Chase recognized that response. He had it himself, as did Yuma. Some life experiences taught it to you.

"What's wrong?" Wendy asked. "Cait?"

Rory nodded and stepped back from her sister. "Her breathing sounds funny. She's warm."

Wendy immediately slipped in beside Cait and leaned forward, putting her ear to Cait's lips. Then she touched Cait's forehead and checked her pulse at her throat.

"There's a bit of congestion. It might just be from sleeping too much. The warmth isn't much yet. It could be from the blankets and the hat."

Rory leaned back against the edge of a seat, almost sagging. "What do we do?"

"We're going to have to try to wake her. Get her to cough." Wendy peeled the blankets back from Cait's chest and pressed her ear there, first one side and then the other. "My kingdom for a stethoscope," she muttered as she leaned back, squatting. "It doesn't sound bad, mostly bronchial congestion. I don't hear anything from lower. But she needs to cough. Apparently, her breathing has been too depressed for too long. We need to clear her out."

Rory stripped off her jacket and gloves fast, then pulled the blankets away from Cait enough to grab her under the arms and lift her.

Cait weighed next to nothing, as Chase knew, but he was still impressed with how easily Rory lifted her sister. Then, holding her with one arm, she began to pat Cait's back. "Cait. Cait! Wake up."

Wendy stepped up, fisted her hand and gave Cait a couple of good thumps on the upper back with the heel of her fist.

Cait's eyes fluttered. "Wha—"

"You need to cough, Cait," Rory said firmly. "We're helping you."

Wendy gave her a couple more thumps. Cait's breathing changed, and now even Chase could hear a rattle from where he was standing. "It's coming," Wendy said.

"Should I put her on the bed?" Rory asked.

"Only if this doesn't work. Just make sure you haven't got her so tight she can't draw air deeply."

A couple more thumps, then a cough. A good cough.

"There we go," Wendy said. "Set her on the seat, let her lean forward a bit. I'm going to get her to express some more."

A few minutes later Wendy was happy with the sound of Cait's breathing. And Cait herself was awake enough to show some interest in tea and soup.

Chase quietly let himself into the cockpit and closed the door. He sat in his seat, staring at the red light and the snow in his cockpit windows that reflected it, dim though it was.

He'd understood that they were working with a time frame when it came to Cait. Four days of medicines. He could tell how frail she was. But what hadn't crossed his mind was the fact that she could get sick with something else and die on this damn plane.

He hadn't thought about pneumonia.

There was a helluva lot he hadn't thought about, and right now he wanted to kick himself hard. Instead he opened his toolbox, got down on the deck and used a flashlight to try to see his way around the wiring for the satellite-comm link.

Waiting out this storm wasn't going to cut it. That was now eminently clear.

Winter nights were naturally long, especially this far north, but Rory felt this one dragging painfully. Occasionally the plane juddered from the wind, and once or twice an eerie moan managed to emerge from the twisted metal. But they didn't slide or tip, and beyond that she didn't care.

She cared about only one thing—her sister. She sat across from Cait, watching her constantly, wishing there was anything more she could do right now. The merciless storm continued to howl, however, and it was so dark out there anyway that even if it quieted they wouldn't be going anywhere.

Cait woke periodically, and each time she did, Rory or Wendy encouraged her to cough, and filled her with more tea and soup, as much as they could get her to swallow. Cait's cooperation was frighteningly listless, as if she drank and coughed only because she knew they wouldn't let her refuse.

Rory caught some uneasy, disturbed sleep, waking at nearly every little sound. She heard the murmurs of Yuma and Chase in the cockpit as they worked on the electronics, and wondered how much either of them knew.

Finally, satisfied that Cait had managed to swallow another cup of heavily sweetened tea, and that she had coughed enough to make her breathing sound clear, she watched her sister drift again into sleep and made her way forward. Both men were lying on the cockpit floor, corkscrewed around the seats, with wires dangling from beneath the console.

"Need any help?" Rory asked.

"I wish," Chase answered. "Apart from lack of room, we're looking at spaghetti here."

A flashlight illuminated a number of loose-leaf manuals between them, and the dangling wires.

"Did you find anything broken?"

"Nope. Everything seems to be connected so far, and we're not disconnecting anything. First rule…"

"Yeah," Yuma said. "If it ain't broke, don't fix it."

"There might have been internal damage to some of the units from impact," Rory remarked.

"That's our concern," Chase agreed. "Although you'd think my damn emergency beacon would be up to it. Still, there's the GPS connection. That's a separate unit, and it could have been damaged. Or it may just be the storm. I'm beginning to think we won't know for sure until we get some clearing."

At that moment, Wendy popped her head over Rory's shoulder. "You know, you two… and by *you two* I mean Chase and Rory…you ought to get some sleep. Yuma can watch over things, and I can watch over Cait, but neither of you will be worth a damn when this storm blows out if you haven't slept."

Rory started to argue, but Wendy was having none of it. She tugged Rory's arm and pulled her back to the aft bedroom where the two twin beds abutted the sides of the plane. "Sleep," she said. "It's our watch now. And you don't want to be useless to your sister."

It was that last argument that worked. Edgy though she felt, Rory gave in, removing her boots and snowpants so she could crawl under the blankets. She was sure she wouldn't sleep, but she began to drift off almost immediately, only vaguely aware that Chase at some point crawled into the other bed.

She was worn out. Everything had worn her out. She hadn't slept well or much since coming home from Mexico to find out how ill her sister was. At least now, with a snowstorm paralyzing them, sleep didn't feel like such a huge waste of time.

When sleep at last arrived, a few rare tears dampened her cheeks.

* * *

Her dreams were disturbed, more memories than dreams, really. She awoke sometime later, while it was still dark, the bedroom illuminated only faintly by the candles that burned in the main cabin.

Back here it had grown cold, so cold that she was curled up in a tight ball with her teeth chattering. She needed to get up, go into the main cabin and seek what warmth she could.

But her mind had hit the ground running, full of thoughts of Cait, of her dire diagnosis, of the fact that the doctors in Seattle could offer no hope this time, except for the trial of a new drug.

Last time had been so different. Nearly four years ago, the doctors had used upbeat words like, *nonaggressive, high cure* and *remission rates.* Yes, there had always been a possibility that the disease could kill her, but their attitudes had been optimistic.

Not now. By the time she had reached the hospital hallways from Mexico, the words that had been flying around were *grave, aggressive, maybe a few months.*

Then one oncologist, a man who never pulled his punches, had said simply, "Your sister's only hope is a trial they're running on a new drug. Do you want me to pull strings and see if I can get her in? I can't make any promises, but they've had some good results with remission."

Because remission was now probably the best Cait could hope for, a few more years disease-free. No one seemed to think there might be a cure anymore. Not now that she had relapsed into an even worse form of the illness.

But Rory wasn't one to give up. She wasn't going to turn precious minutes of Cait's life over to the Grim

Reaper without a fight...even if Cait herself didn't seem to want to fight anymore.

And that son of a bitch Hal had deprived her of hope. He couldn't handle having a sick wife again. At least that was his excuse. Rory suspected he'd been cheating on Cait for a long time, maybe since she first got ill. According to one of the nurses she'd spoken to out of concern for Cait's despair, that wasn't uncommon. Apparently "till death do us part" didn't mean much in the case of lingering illness.

"I see it lots of times," the nurse had said bluntly. "And the ones who stick around ogle me like fresh meat and flirt with me. Right in front of their wives. You ask me, a lot of men just aren't any good for the long haul."

"But you see others who stick it out?" Rory had asked, maybe because she wanted to strangle Hal.

"Sure. There are good men. Just not as many as you would hope. Not when it comes to this."

So Hal was just an ordinary creep, no worse than most of his kind, not as good as some. But part of what maddened Rory the most was the way it had cut the heart out of Cait. No pep talks worked. No desire to get even and show her husband inspired her.

Cait had just plain given up. Life had become a load too heavy to carry anymore. And Rory, who felt an unnatural urge to violence when it came to Cait's husband, restrained herself because even she could see that the damage had been done and there was nothing on earth that would repair the wound.

Except time. But Cait was dreadfully short on time now.

Another tear leaked out from one eye, almost fiery in its warmth against the chill of her cheeks. She couldn't afford this sorrow and weakness—she had to take care of Cait. Later, if nothing worked, would come the time to grieve. But not now, not while Cait still needed her.

Another shiver ripped through her, and she clamped her teeth to still their chattering. It *had* to be warmer in the cabin.

Before she could move, she saw a familiar shape move in the dim glow of the candlelight from the cabin, then Chase bent down near her ear.

"I can hear you shivering. Scoot over."

"I should check Cait."

"I just looked out. Wendy's wide awake, sitting right across from her. Look, your getting hypothermic isn't going to help anyone."

She couldn't argue the basic sense of that, so she scooted over. He'd doffed his jacket and boots, and soon she was cradled against his heat, his strength beneath the blanket. Great strength, she realized as he nestled her head on his sweatshirt-covered shoulder and pulled her close to his chest.

The muscles she felt flexing against her were the hard, flat muscles of hard work, not the bulging carefully cultivated masterpieces some men liked. She'd quit going to co-ed gyms years ago because she had gotten tired of watching men work their pectorals and biceps as if they were the only muscles that mattered.

Of course, when she was in the field, she saw plenty of hardworking muscle, especially on hot days, but she didn't feel it pressed up against her, holding her. Indeed, she'd gotten to where she hardly noticed it. But this was different.

Chase was so warm. Almost too soon, it seemed, his heat began to penetrate her, reaching deep inside, thawing her bones, easing her tension, halting the shivering. Then it filled her not only with comfort, but with a sweet yearning she had almost forgotten existed.

She turned her head a little so she could press her eyes to his shoulder and try to stave off the tears. She didn't cry. She wasn't a crier by nature and hadn't been since childhood. But now she wanted to cry, just sob her eyes out.

She was just worn out, she told herself. It had been a hard few weeks, finding out how sick Cait was, and then trying to find a miracle for her, or at least the hope of one. Exhaustion had weakened her, that was all.

Exhaustion and fear. Because being forced to sit here and do nothing in a crashed plane while her sister's life was waning by the minute was almost more than she could stand. Yet every ounce of common sense argued against every emotion that demanded she do *something*. Doing something right now would be foolhardy.

"You're tensing again," he murmured.

So he wasn't sleeping. Then his hands began to rub her back gently, soothingly.

"Your sister?" he asked.

"Every minute of every day," she admitted.

"Understandable. And being stuck like this has got to be a nightmare for you."

She couldn't deny that, so she didn't bother. It *was* a nightmare, just like the ones she had as a child when something was chasing her and she couldn't move.

"I can't find a problem with the GPS," he remarked. "I don't see any damage, the wiring to it seems fine, so we just have to hope we're not getting signal because of the storm."

"But it could be something you can't see."

She gave him credit for not hesitating. She hated it when she suspected people of trying not to be totally truthful. "It could be. There was a time when anyone who was handy could fix just about anything. Then they came up with black boxes."

She nodded a little against his shoulder, relieved to realize that the urge to weep was fading. Maybe his hand rubbing her back had something to do with that. Or maybe it was thinking about the other problems they faced. She always felt better when she had the true measure of a situation. It always made her feel more in control, and provided an opportunity to think of solutions. She was a born problem-solver.

"Lots of black boxes," she admitted. "Microminiaturization—the curse of modern life."

"Sometimes it is."

"When something breaks, it is. If you can get to a store for a replacement, no problem. On the side of a mountain in a blizzard, big problem."

"Unfortunately. Regardless, I won't be able to say for sure until the storm lets up. With any luck, we'll pick up signal, the beacon will start broadcasting our position, and we'll be airlifted out of here in a matter of hours."

"And if it doesn't?"

"Then we'll damn well start down the mountainside. I mean it, Rory."

"I know you do." She didn't doubt it. "It might be best for me to stay here with Cait if you do. I'm not sure she could survive a trip like that."

"No. Absolutely not. This plane is going to be invisible under the snow. There's no guarantee if some of us start down the mountain that we'd be able to guide searchers back here quickly enough. We go together or we stay together."

"I'm thinking of exposure."

"And I'm thinking of lost time."

Both of which could kill Cait. The ultimate rock and a hard place. "I know. Trust me, I know."

"I'm sure you do. With any luck, we won't have to make the decision either way."

A quiet snort escaped her. "I'm not feeling very lucky right now. Are you?"

A couple of heartbeats passed before he answered. She knew because she could hear the quiet, steady beating of his heart, a reassuring sound. "I wasn't at first. I mean, if I hadn't just had this bird in for an overhaul, I wouldn't feel quite as furious about a mechanical failure. It shouldn't have happened."

"No, it most definitely shouldn't have."

"But," he said, emphasizing the word, "I'm feeling lucky anyway, because given that something went wrong and we lost our engines, it's damn near a miracle no one was hurt."

"True."

"So tell yourself that miracles happen, Rory. And we might be entitled to more than one. Especially given that we shouldn't be here at all."

Her throat tightened and she had to swallow several times before she could answer. Her voice remained a bit husky. "I hope you're right. Are you always so upbeat?"

"The alternative sure isn't any help."

"No." She knew he was right, but at the moment she was finding it hard to feel upbeat about Cait's plight. That would come back as soon as she could take some action again. In the meantime, she wanted to think about something else before the black trickle of despair she felt grew into an ocean. "Was it hard flying without the engines?"

"Not fun," he said, still keeping his voice down.

"We were slightly more aerodynamic than a boulder. Just slightly. Our remaining airspeed was all that gave me any maneuverability and the more that dropped the harder it got."

"But the wings have enough lift that the wind was trying to pick them up."

"That's the wings. And the air has to move across them fast enough to create enough lift for an aircraft this heavy. You remember Bernoulli."

She did, vaguely. "My education has mostly been in rocks."

"Then you would have felt right at home in the cockpit for a while there."

The humor surprised her, touched her and actually lifted her spirits a bit. "Until I got out my rock hammer," she tried to joke back.

"I was sure ready to hammer something. I just didn't have time."

Finally, she said what she should have said hours ago, most especially sure it was true and she should have been grateful rather than angry as she had been initially. "Thanks for getting us down in one piece."

"You can thank me when we're all safely out of here."

"No, I don't think so."

He shifted a little. "What do you mean?" He actually sounded uncomfortable.

"Whether we get out of here or not, there wouldn't even be a question of survival if you weren't a damn good pilot. So thanks for giving me the opportunity to worry some more."

"Sure. I think."

"I'm serious."

"I know." Again that uncomfortable shifting. "So what's the story with Cait? Has she been sick for long?"

"She got nonaggressive NHL a few years back and they managed to put her into remission. The stats are actually pretty good for that."

"But it's aggressive now?"

Rory had to swallow before she could speak. Her throat was tightening up again, and she hoped he couldn't hear it. She didn't want to seem weak. "Yeah. Very. And since her husband left her when she got sick again, I don't think she wants to live."

He swore quietly. "Well, that sure as hell complicates things, doesn't it?"

"A whole lot."

"And there's an experimental treatment in Minnesota?"

"Yeah. She was sinking so fast it was hard to get her in."

"And now this."

"Now this."

He muttered another curse. "I'm sorry, Rory."

"It's not your fault. At first I was mad, sure you must have done something wrong, but from what you've told me, it sounds like some mechanic did something wrong. At least we're all okay. And somehow we'll get out of this."

"Because we have to."

She noted that he said it as if it was all the reason he needed. Just *have to*. Well, there'd been plenty of times in her own life when forced to take action had been all that had kept her going and moving mountains. This was just another mountain, more frightening and intimidating than most, but still just a mountain.

"You must be scared," he said, surprising her.

"I am." It was easy enough to admit. "The treatment might not work. I know that. Not at this stage. But I think it'd have a whole lot better chance if she *wanted* to live."

"Well, of course. I don't suppose there's any chance her husband will come to his senses?"

"I doubt it. He moved in with one of his graduate students. I really don't think Cait would want him back now anyway."

"Probably not. I wouldn't, in her shoes. And I've been in her shoes, sort of."

The admission surprised her. "Really? You? The hunky flying ace?"

A startled but quiet laugh escaped him. "Try living with a navy pilot. Gone six months at a stretch. Sometimes flying in dangerous parts of the world. Looks good until you have to live it. And there's a lot of temptation around a base when your significant other is gone. Besides, I never got far enough that I felt I had an exclusive claim."

"I take it you've been on the curb more than once."

"More than once," he said frankly. "Which leads me to believe I'm not easy to get along with anyway. And maybe I wasn't back then. There's a sort of cockiness that goes with the job, I admit."

"And now?"

"If I have any cockiness left, I haven't noticed it recently. Flying a taxi kind of puts you in your place, don't you think?"

"Depends on who's hiring you." She rolled her head a bit, surveying the glow from the cabin, trying to see his face and being rewarded with a view of his chin. "You don't like what you're doing now?"

"What I like is flying. I've always loved it. And I've

discovered that I don't have to be in dogfights, or pull five Gs in a roll to enjoy it. So these days I think of myself as carrying eggs."

"Eggs?" she chuckled.

"Eggs," he repeated. "Raw eggs. And my job is to give them such a smooth ride their shells remain intact. That's not always easy flying over the mountains." He shifted a bit, and somehow he was holding her a little closer. "I guess it's all a matter of attitude."

She nodded against his shoulder, agreeing. Warmth had permeated every corner of her body, even her toes, and now that the cold was no longer a threat she was noticing other things, things she hadn't paid attention to in a long time now.

Like how good a man could smell—especially this one. She felt guilty for letting herself grow aware of him. For God's sake, Cait was in the cabin, so sick… Guilt started to rise in a nauseating wave. Then she realized something. Right now she couldn't do even the least thing for Cait. Nothing. Wendy was sitting out there, a trained and experienced nurse. Better care, no doubt, than she herself could provide.

So what was wrong with letting go for just a few minutes? Nothing. Maybe she needed it for her sanity after the last few weeks, a few minutes of escape into fantasy.

Because it was pure fantasy. When they got out of here, she'd be headed to Minnesota and would never see this man again.

That thought made it even more tempting to indulge the images that had begun to dance around the edges of her mind. He continued to rub her back, but she imagined her sweater vanished. She knew how his palm felt already, warm and dry, and it was easy to imagine it running up and down her back, skin on skin.

She felt her nipples pebble with hunger, and as they did so, a shaft of longing speared straight to her loins. Wow. It seemed like forever since she had responded to nothing but a few stray thoughts. Given her job, she'd carved sex right out of her life. She couldn't afford to have her subordinates gossiping and certainly not the roughnecks she worked with. Becoming asexual had seemed like a necessary protective mechanism.

But she didn't need that protection right now, and long-buried needs struggled within her for recognition.

He smelled good. He felt good against her. Knowing absolutely nothing could happen right now made her feel safe, too. With eyes closed, her senses filled with him, she let the fantasy train roll out of the station.

She hovered on the cusp of anticipation, caught on a needlepoint of longing as she imagined him transgressing beyond the gentle backrub. What if he slipped his hand around and cupped her breast? An electric shock zapped through her at the mere idea of how it would feel to have him touch her there, even through layers of clothing. Between her legs, a weight grew, heavy and hungry, and began to throb damply.

So far so fast, she thought with amazement. One little wisp of fantasy and she was as ready as she had ever been in her life. She bit her lower lip, tensing inwardly against the yearning that might cause her to make a betraying move. Thank goodness he couldn't read her mind. That privacy was precious, and she didn't want to reveal her thoughts by slipping and moving in some revealing way.

But oh, she wished she could. Her heart sped a bit and she bit her lip harder. If only this were the time and place, she'd gladly indulge in a quick, meaningless mating just to satisfy the hunger and carry a memory of it with her.

Memories served her well when she was far from home, and a stash of them that involved having hot, impatient sex with Chase seemed worth putting in her mental photo album.

It would be so easy. All she had to do was lean a little closer, roll just enough to throw her leg over his, and the invitation would be unmistakable.

Then, a few minor adjustments of clothing. They wouldn't even need to disrobe completely. Quick, hot… and frankly more like something you'd get on a street corner in many of the towns she'd seen.

A sigh almost slipped out of her as the fantasy popped, leaving her feeling disappointed and frustrated. That wasn't her—rough and ready, mating with a stranger. What was wrong with her? But that's exactly the urge he'd awakened in her, however briefly.

Stress, she told herself. Too much stress and worry. She was losing it.

Then he astonished her by the simple expedient of stroking her hair back from her forehead. She kept her hair relatively short because washing it wasn't easy in some of the places she worked, and it had been a long time since anyone had seemed interested in running their fingers through it.

But he did, combing the soft curls with his fingers, then once again slowly running his hand down her neck and her back. A shiver trickled through her, and it was not the cold.

"Sleep," he whispered. "Wendy will call you if Cait needs you. But you need to sleep."

So did he, she thought. Then, unconsciously, she

snuggled closer, letting him make her feel safe and wanted, illusion though it was, and this time when she closed her eyes, no tears fell and sleep came quietly.

Chapter 5

"Rory?"

She woke from a sleep so dreamless and deep that she almost felt drugged. Chase was still holding her, but it was his voice that had called to her.

"Mmm?" Her eyelids felt heavier than lead.

"Cait's asking for you."

All of a sudden, the lead vanished from her eyes and the sleep from her body. She sat up so fast she almost banged her head on the curving fuselage beside her.

"Whoa," Chase said. "Don't hurt yourself. That's a complication none of us needs."

Even as he spoke, though, he was sliding out of the bed, pulling the covers back so she could climb out. At once she noted how chilly the air felt after the warm cocoon Chase had made for her. No time for that now.

Except Chase figured there was time. "Get your boots on," he said. "You can't afford to get cold."

He was probably right about that. Between time and the risk of hypothermia, this plane wasn't as cozy as it might seem. Cozier than being totally exposed, but hardly a safe haven.

She jammed her feet into her boots, then reached for the laces as the light brightened and she realized that someone had brought a candle into the room. She glanced up long enough to see that it was Chase.

"It's not an emergency," he said, reassuring her. "She just asked for you. Wendy doesn't seem worried."

"Right." As if she'd take anyone else's word for that, except a doctor, and then only a doctor who had a chance to get to know all details of Cait's medical history. Nothing against Wendy, but she hadn't even known Cait twenty-four hours yet, and had no medical records to refer to. Those had all been faxed ahead.

She finished tying her boots then stood, reaching for her parka. Chase moved out of the way so she could stride quickly into the cabin as she pulled her jacket on.

She found Cait bundled in the same seat. Wendy had evidently lowered the back for her at some point, nearly making it flat, although she'd kept Cait's torso elevated by a few inches.

Rory squatted beside her and laid her hand on Cait's shoulder. "How are you doing, sweetie?"

"Okay." Cait's eyes fluttered with weariness, but she managed a faint smile. "They didn't have to wake you."

"They knew I'd want them to. Nobody risks my wrath."

Cait's smile deepened a shade. "Not even when we were little."

"Not even then," Rory agreed. "Are you hungry? How about something to drink? Something hot?"

"Wendy's been taking good care of me. Just sit with me?"

"Sure." Moving carefully, Rory stepped over her sister to the adjoining seat next to the window. All the blinds had been pulled down—not that it mattered. There was probably not a thing to see out there except snow.

She smiled at Wendy. "Your turn to get some sleep."

"I'm not going to pass on that offer. Billy Joe?"

He poked his head out of the cockpit. "Yo?"

"It's our turn for bed."

"Damn that sounds good."

Rory watched the Yumas work their way to the back of the plane and slipped her hand under blankets until she found Cait's hand and was able to hold it. She was grateful to discover that her sister's fingers didn't feel icy.

Chase moved around the cabin, replacing some old candles with new ones, and even added a few more to hold back the cold. The cabin wasn't freezing, by any means, but it wasn't toasty, either. Blankets and lots of clothing were necessary.

But it *was* warmer than the bedroom, and Rory was grateful that they had moved Cait out here. As sick as she was, she didn't have the stamina to withstand the cold, or much in the way of stressors. If they had to try to carry her out of here in order to save her life, they'd be risking it, as well.

Suddenly Cait's fingers tightened around hers. "Rory? Don't worry so much about me. It's in God's hands."

"That's the part I'm having trouble with."

"You always have." Cait's voice grew fainter, as if speaking were an effort. But her eyes remained open, looking at Rory. Then, slowly, they tracked to Chase. "You're the pilot, right?"

Chase slid into the seat facing her. "That's right, ma'am. Blame it all on me."

"I think you're a good pilot. We're still alive." A smile flickered around Cait's pale lips. "What's that saying?"

"A good landing," he replied, "is any landing you can walk away from."

"That's it. Very true." Then her eyelids sagged and she slipped again into sleep.

Rory turned her attention to Chase and found him frowning at Cait. He seemed to sense her attention, because he looked at her. "We'll get her to that hospital," he said quietly. "If I have to carry her out of here on my back."

Rory nodded, her throat tightening, even though she knew that might be too much for Cait. But if there was no alternative...

Ah, she couldn't think about that now. One foot in front of the other. How many times in life had she needed to do that? It ought to be a lesson well-learned.

"Rory?" Cait had apparently only been dozing lightly.

"Hmm?"

"Remember Mom and Dad?"

"Of course."

"I never told you, but I wanted to be like them. I shouldn't have gotten married...." Then she trailed off as she fell back to sleep.

That was surely one of the saddest statements she'd ever heard her sister make, enough to clamp a vice around her chest. Rory looked over and found Chase's eyes questioning her. She needed a moment to find the breath to respond.

"Our parents were both doctors. Once we grew up, they started working in underdeveloped countries with an international organization."

"That's impressive."

"Yeah. Except it killed them."

His brows drew together. "How?"

"They both caught a rare hemorrhagic fever and died. Five years ago. Right before Cait started to get sick."

"I'm sorry."

"That's life." Her mantra, although it was getting harder to say of late. *Life is unfair,* she reminded herself for the hundredth time. "They knew the risks, we discussed them, I was proud of what they wanted to do. And they weren't the only people who died in that outbreak. Lots of other grieving families."

"Does it help to think of it that way?"

Rory shrugged one shoulder. "Not always. But Cait is all I have left to call family. She loved her husband. I can't tell you how it hurts to hear her say she should never have married. That bastard deserves some comeuppance."

"From you?"

She shook her head. "No. I don't deal in vengeance. Which is not to say I wouldn't like to—I just don't do it. It would bring me down to his level."

"And you're better than that?"

"I wouldn't say that. But I try to be."

Chase nodded. "That's the key, I think. Trying to be better people." Then he gave her a crooked smile as if to lighten the mood. "I have the skinned knees and elbows to show for my attempts."

It worked. She felt herself smiling back a little. Just a little. Cait's hand within hers stirred a bit, then quieted. Still warm.

"So your parents were medical missionaries?"

"No, not like that. They worked for a private foundation, purely secular. They paid their own travel and living expenses and worked as volunteers. Sometimes, I guess, they even bought medicine and equipment."

"Pretty noble. Interesting that Cait mentioned that now."

Rory thought so, too. She looked at Cait and wondered if her younger sister had always harbored such a desire, and falling in love had simply gotten in the way, or if this was something new. Rory had moved on to jobs far away by the time Cait got married, and had been in touch with her sister mostly during holidays while Cait was still in high school. Neither of them had been good correspondents, satisfied to send a single line of email, and Cait had been awfully busy, too. Friends, school activities, a very full social calendar.

"She was a lot more outgoing than me," Rory said, still watching her sister, remembering. "I was more of a nerd, always buried in a book or a project. My idea of a great summer was hiking around some mountains and mapping things."

"Not looking for oil?"

"Not always. Sometimes I just enjoyed the rocks, and figuring out how things had come to be. Oil became my business later." She looked at him. "What about you?"

"Well, I can't remember a time when I didn't want to fly. I don't think I left room for much else. If flying required being good at math, then I'd be good at math. That was the way I thought. For a while I had a thing for fast cars, but that got in the way of what I needed to do to get into the academy so I gave it up."

"You're an academy grad?"

"Ring-knocker, that's me."

"I'm impressed."

He winked. "You'll get over it."

"Probably," she admitted, smiling. "Where did that term come from anyway?"

"Academy class rings. I think it was a derogatory way of saying those who graduated from the academies never let it be forgotten. It's an old term, though. I haven't heard it in a while." He shook his head a little, appearing amused. "I'm sure they've come up with better ones."

"People usually do when they resent something. I hear the academy is rough."

"Mostly in the first year. Then it gets better."

He didn't seem to want to go into it, so she didn't press him anymore. Heck, it wasn't as if she wanted to sit here and reminisce about *her* college days. She looked at Cait, glad to see that her sister appeared to be sleeping comfortably.

College seemed like an awfully long time ago now. The thought was almost wistful. "Things were so much simpler back then," she murmured. "In college, I mean. I had so much hope, everything seemed possible."

"Yeah."

"Funny how we don't often appreciate things until we're past them. All those big, important things that concerned me back then? I'd switch them for the problems right now in a heartbeat."

"I think a lot of us would. Maybe it says something that our view of what's a problem changes as we get older."

A sigh escaped her. "Too true. They do seem to get bigger and harder."

Cait murmured quietly and turned a little toward Rory. The movement made Rory's heart squeeze. How long did she have left with Cait? A few hours, a few days, a few weeks? Not long unless the experimental treatment worked. Not long before she might lose the last of her family on this earth.

She had to look away for fear that Chase would see the tears that had begun to sting her eyes. Didn't want him to guess how afraid she was, or that for the last few weeks she'd been so angry that she could barely stand herself.

But apparently she hadn't looked away fast enough, because she heard Chase move, and the next thing she knew he had captured her free hand in both of his. Reluctantly, she looked at him.

"We're going to get her out of here if there's any way humanly possible. I swear it."

She managed a nod. Then she admitted something she hadn't said out loud, not once. "I hate myself."

"Why?"

"Because I wasn't here. Because I was bouncing around the world doing my thing, and I lost all that time with my sister. I've hardly been back to see her since she was sick last time, and before that…not much better."

He stayed quiet for a while, not replying. But maybe there was nothing anyone could say. She'd screwed up. She'd gone off to live her own life without considering just how short life could be, especially so for her kid sister. Even after the last round, once Cait was in remission, she'd taken off again. She had promised herself she'd come home to visit every few months, but she hadn't. She had failed to learn the lesson.

"I'm stupid," she said. "How many times do I need to be beaten over the head? Our parents died, then Cait got sick, and what do I do? As soon as the docs said Cait was in remission I went back to my old globe-trotting ways."

"What were you supposed to do?" he asked. "Stop living your own life and move in next door?"

"No, but I should have come back more often. I should have gotten the message that tomorrows aren't guaranteed."

"No, they're not. But most of us couldn't survive if we believed that. Counting on tomorrow is what keeps us going. And you had your own life, Rory. You were entitled to that. You didn't do anything wrong."

"I think I did."

"Okay. But look at you now. You've dropped everything. I'm assuming that doing that has messed with your career a bit, since most people can't just drop out of their jobs for weeks on end. I know I couldn't. If I did what you're doing, I'd practically have to rebuild my business from the ground up."

"It's not quite that bad."

"*Quite,* huh. That tells me it is. But you didn't hesitate, you came home to take care of your sister, and you're not counting the cost. I can tell that from the fact that you hired me to get you halfway across the country to get her an experimental treatment. A lot of people wouldn't do that. So quit beating yourself up. You're here when she needs you."

"Late, but yeah." He was making sense, but the sense wasn't reaching her heart. She *did* appreciate the way he held her hand, though, and inevitably thought back to the time they had spent bundled in the bunk while he warmed her up. Her cheeks burned a bit as she remembered her burgeoning fantasies about him, and then it struck her that he was a generous man. He hadn't hesitated to offer his body heat when he surely must have been more comfortable in his own bunk than holding a stiff, shivering woman. And while that might be simply a matter of survival imperative, he hadn't been required to move over her way and take her hand when he sensed her emotional distress. Hell, most of the men she knew ran like sprinters from that sort of thing.

In fact, in her job she'd had to become "one of the guys," so much so that she never showed any emotion other than anger or humor. It almost surprised her to realize the tenderhearted part of her still existed.

It surprised her almost as much to realize that she wasn't exactly comfortable with it anymore, either. She wanted to fight for Cait with everything she had. She found it easy to get angry at the illness, easy to swing into action to reach for a last straw. What was not easy any longer was feeling the aching love for her sister, her fears, her pain.

Her job had warped her, she guessed, but she wasn't sure that was a bad thing. However it turned out with Cait, at some point she was going back to those oil fields and the world of machismo.

She drew a deep breath, not exactly a sigh, and waited for her internal landscape to resettle into more familiar contours. She couldn't afford to let herself fall apart. Not now, for Cait's sake. Later, for her own.

With effort, she removed her hand from Chase's clasp, regretting the loss of contact immediately, but steeling herself against it. She leaned back a little in her chair, and he read her reaction accurately. At once he leaned back in his own seat, and the gulf between them widened.

"Sleep if you want," he said to her. "I can keep an eye on things."

"You need sleep, too," she said. "We need you in top form. I'm no survivalist." A logical explanation when in truth she just didn't want to be unfair or selfish. They were supposed to share these watches.

He nodded. "Call me if you need anything." Then he rose and went to the cockpit.

Leaving her feeling alone all of a sudden.

Don't, she told herself. *Don't go there.* Given the circumstances, for all she knew she was experiencing some variant of the Stockholm syndrome, where hostages become attached to their captors. What did she know about this guy, anyway? That he had a military background? That the Yumas had been his friends for a long time? That under these circumstances he could be generous? What about the rest of the time?

He had already admitted that he didn't succeed at long-term relationships, that he was often, if not always, dumped. That should be a red flag.

Yet as she looked at herself she saw the same experience. She hadn't had anything approaching a long-term relationship since college, and in retrospect she could see that it had been motivated more by raging hormones than anything else.

Her life now didn't leave room for the long term. She traveled too much, and spent most of her life in places where she couldn't establish a relationship that wouldn't interfere with her job, or the perception of her workers.

In her experience, too, she seemed to intimidate a lot of men. High drive and career preoccupation, not to mention being home only a few weeks a year, didn't seem to appeal to the kinds of men who wanted more than a quick roll in the hay.

So who was she to think Chase's track record meant he was somehow defective? Thinking about it, she could easily see that, being gone for such long periods, he'd be leaving behind girlfriends who would face a lot of temptation around military bases. Guys who were actually there. Unless the relationship evolved into something strong and permanent, it would be unlikely to survive.

As for him having been cocky, well, she could imagine that might almost be a prerequisite for a military pilot. What else would make you take those chances again and again?

She smothered a sigh and looked at Cait, acknowledging that thinking about who Chase was or wasn't was a form of escape from her worry and fear. Much easier to ponder the characteristics of a near stranger than to actually think about how her sister's life was hanging by a thread.

A thread made all the thinner because she seemed to have given up.

Sometimes Rory almost wanted to shake Cait, to tell her there was a life apart from Hal. But she didn't have the right to do that. She couldn't even address it from experience. She had no personal knowledge of what it was like to love a man enough to marry him and devote your life to him. To be dumped by him when you'd given him everything, all because you were sick. To be abandoned by love at the moment when you most needed it.

Maybe she should get a voodoo doll of Hal and stick pins in it.

Impotent anger seemed to ride her constantly and

she hated it. At work she could solve nearly any problem. Now she was facing one she might not be able to do a damn thing about.

The experimental treatment had been a slim straw. Now that straw was slipping away as they sat mired in a blizzard inside a crashed plane. It seemed as if life knew no mercy.

Was she becoming bitter, too?

But reality was looking ugly right now. Her parents had devoted their lives to doing good for the less fortunate, and had died because of it. Now her sister, who had devoted her life to a man, and dreams of a family with him, had been abandoned in her hour of need.

Where was the good stuff? Did everything you reached for only turn to pain and loss?

Yeah, she understood that bad things happened to good people. She wasn't naïve. Her sister, and millions of others like her, didn't deserve to get hit with such serious illness. Stuff like that just happened, governed by the randomness of fate. She got that. It wasn't about what you deserved.

Meteors fell from the sky, too, and once in a while they hit a person. Maybe the amazing thing was that they didn't hit more people.

But sometimes, if you turned that pattern of random events around in your mind and looked at it from another angle, it didn't look quite so random, and so you started asking the unanswerable cosmic question: *Why?*

Her mother had talked to her about that once when she was in high school, and the words had stayed with her. She could hear it as if her mother were sitting right beside her:

Honey, bad things happen to everyone. It's what we

*learn from them that determines whether we become
better people or worse people.*

Was she in danger of becoming worse? Because
she didn't feel like she was especially good as it was.
Nor could she ignore that very bitter rat now gnawing
around the edges of her thoughts.

She stopped another sigh, looked at Cait's pale, small
face. Her sister had become a mere shadow of herself,
looking almost waiflike in her weakness. So fragile she
reminded Rory of a dandelion puff, something a mere
breath of air could scatter and carry away.

It shocked her.

Working around roughnecks in oil fields had taught
her just how tough the human body was, how much re-
silience it truly possessed. It took a lot to actually kill
a man.

Then this. Her sister exemplified the opposite side of
the coin—displaying just how fragile life really could
be. How frighteningly frail.

Just as morbid thoughts threatened to consume her,
the plane jerked and let out a groan like a dying giant.

Rory froze, looking quickly at Cait, but Cait barely
stirred. *My God, what was that?*

At once Chase emerged from the cockpit and started
reaching for his outerwear. An instant later, Wendy and
Yuma joined them.

"What was that?" Rory asked

"I think we just moved. I need to check it out." Chase
pulled on his jacket impatiently.

"I'll go with you," Yuma said instantly. "You
shouldn't go alone."

"No, you stay. You're the only other one of us with
survival experience in these mountains, plus you know

your way around the GPS and beacon controls. If both you and I go out there we could endanger everyone."

"I'll go," Rory said. "Yuma's right. In these conditions no one should go out alone." She looked at Wendy. "You know where Cait's meds are?"

Wendy nodded. "I saw."

Even as she yanked on her outerwear, Rory wondered if she was doing the right thing. She hated to leave Cait in someone else's care, but it would be foolhardy for Chase to go into this blizzard alone. And if someone could take care of Cait, it was certainly Wendy.

They couldn't afford to risk losing anyone to this storm, but a long career of making hard-eyed risk assessments told her that she was the most expendable of the lot. Another uncomfortable thought, but an honest one.

She felt a flicker of dark amusement. Funny how coming up against life and death made you realize just how puny and unimportant you were.

As soon as they were tightly buttoned up in their cold-weather gear, she and Chase both grabbed flashlights. Getting the door open seemed a little harder, as if the metal of the plane had twisted more, but with a couple of shoves it opened.

Outside the weather had grown savage. Rory felt the wind try to grab her and snatch her as she crawled over the badly angled stairs for the deepening snow outside. At last she stood beside Chase, their flashlights bouncing off wildly swirling snow, and then watched him close up their steel cocoon.

If Mother Nature had temper tantrums, this seemed like one of them. Even inside her snorkel hood the wind tried to steal her breath, and icy needles of flying snow stung her briefly before melting.

"What do you think it was?" she asked again, just as the wind keened forlornly around some obstacle.

"We're going to find out. Grab on to my jacket somewhere and hang on. We don't want to get separated."

No, they didn't. Rory estimated the whiteout conditions were limiting visibility to maybe five feet. She grabbed the bottom hem of Chase's jacket and hung on tight.

Dry though it was, the snow didn't help their footing at all. Obstacles had become invisible, and the ground offered plenty of them, for this was a mountainside—not pavement. Rocks, tree limbs, dips and unexpected hills all made the going tough, as did the wind itself. At times it slapped her so hard she felt like a sail in a gale.

Chase stayed close to the plane, moving slowly, shining his flashlight all over it, from the top of the fuselage, which was almost invisible, to the ground on which it sat.

As they rounded the tail, the plane itself blocked the wind, at least briefly.

"We must have shifted," he said, leaning his head close to hers so she could hear.

"The wind?"

"In part, probably. But you know what happens when ice gets compressed."

"It liquefies."

"Exactly. There was snow here before we came down. I'm guessing that the weight of the plane is melting it. By now we're probably sitting on a layer of ice and water."

That didn't sound very hopeful, but she just nodded her acknowledgment.

"We shouldn't be able to slide too far," he said reassuringly.

She hoped he was right. But she wondered just how much more stress the fuselage could take before it cracked like an eggshell. She imagined it must have been built to endure forces not so very different from the ones she dealt with drilling for oil. All those take-offs and landings, all the buffeting…it was undoubtedly strong. But no one could guess how much metal fatigue it had suffered in this landing.

They worked their way slowly around the other side. He seemed to be looking for worrisome signs of some kind. Perhaps additional buckling that appeared too sharp. The kind of thing that might expose them to the elements. The wing still had airspace beneath it, and she wondered if that was good. The wind must be gusting at least forty miles an hour, not enough for real lift. He was right about that. But maybe enough to move them from time to time.

They eased around the wing, staying close together, and worked their way toward the craft's nose. It was still mostly buried in snow, as it had been from the beginning, but more of the windscreen was visible now. The wind was steadily unburying it. What did that mean?

To her surprise, Chase began to dig away some of the snow with his free hand, revealing more of the nose cone. It looked a bit rumpled but not bad, considering that it had plowed its way through snow and debris. After examining the bit he could see, he patted it, almost fondly, as if pleased with how well it had withstood the landing.

A sudden *whop* caused them both to turn and look

back at the wing. Flying snow almost entirely hid it
from view.

"The wing flexed," he said with a certainty that indicated he'd heard that sound before.

"That's not good. It could move us—that much
energy."

"I know. Let's move farther forward."

She followed him into the maelstrom, hanging on to
the hem of his jacket, noting that he didn't place them
right in front of the plane. So he was indeed afraid that
it might move.

Well, she was, too. They made their way forward
until the nose was almost lost in the snow blowing
behind them.

"You stand here," he said. "Keep your flashlight
pointed in my direction so I can find my way back. I
want to be sure of what exactly is in front of us."

"Okay."

Even inside her snorkel hood, the wind sounded loud,
as did the swishing of snow as it snaked drily across the
surface. Each time the wind twisted around and pushed
at her, she could hear icy crystals pelt the nylon of her
jacket.

Damn, it was cold and dry, and in no time at all she
could tell where Chase was only by the insistent glow
of his flashlight. The snow caught the light and tossed
it around, making it unreliable, but still illuminating
his general direction. It didn't exactly swallow the light,
but it might as well have the way the flakes shattered
the light everywhere in tiny, gleaming pinpricks.

She staggered a bit as the wind hit her back hard.
This was not a great night to be out. The elements were
having their way with everything, and she felt smaller

just then than she ever had. Around her loomed a forest she couldn't see, a night that was full of threat.

The thought of animals didn't unnerve her. Little that lived unnerved her after some of the places she had been, but no animal with any wisdom would be prowling in this storm. No, it was the storm she feared, and how it could worsen their situation.

While the blizzard raged, threatening the plane, inside that plane her sister clung weakly to life. Time and the elements were conspiring, and she had to fight an urge to throw her head back and scream her fear, frustration and fury into the howling storm. As if the elements might heed it.

Almost unbearable tension coiled her muscles, and she'd have given almost anything to have the power to set this all to rights. Never, ever, had she felt so utterly helpless, except perhaps during the mere minutes before that well blew. Oh, hell, that didn't even come close. At least *then* she'd been able to get most of her people away in time.

An eternity seemed to pass, though she was sure it couldn't have been more than ten or fifteen minutes, before Chase began once again to emerge from the swirling snow. First his flashlight, then his vague outline, dark against the whiter snow.

"We can't move far," he told her as he reached her. "Even if there's a ravine up there buried in the snow, we'd probably slide right over it if we skate because it's so narrow."

"But if we don't?"

"Then we're going to be walking uphill inside the plane."

"Could it withstand that?"

"Ordinarily, I'd say yes, but after all this, I honestly don't know."

Icy fingers, icier than the needles of snow that stung her face, gripped her heart. "Can we do anything to prevent it?"

He waved in the general direction of the plane. "What do you think? That bird is heavy."

True. She lowered her head a bit, biting her lip, thinking about all the other dangers that might still get them. No, they couldn't prevent that massive, crippled plane from moving if it decided to. "Beyond the ravine?"

"Woods. They'd stop us for sure. How much damage we'd have would depend on how much momentum we built on a slide."

She turned from him and looked back toward the nearly invisible plane. A lot of momentum, if those tons of aluminum started moving. They wouldn't have to move fast. Hard as it was, they were going to have to trust that the plane would stay put because there wasn't a damn thing they could do to prevent it from moving. "I wish we could do something about the wings."

"Me, too. I don't think they're getting much lift at all, but evidently it's enough to cause them to flex. More metal fatigue."

"Yeah." That was one thing she knew a little about. "I guess we're just going to have to ignore the groans and moans." Not at all comforting, that thought.

"I can't see any other answer."

She'd been out here too long, she realized. Some inner clock was ticking, and it was pushing her to get back to Cait, to make sure she was still all right.

Chase took her elbow this time as they struggled back up alongside the plane. Funny, she hadn't noticed the slope on the way down, but now she felt the climb back up. Maybe they were at a high enough altitude to notice the thinness of the air.

The wing ahead of them flapped again, a strange sort of hollow, metallic sound, followed by a banshee moan. Before Rory even realized what was happening, she had been shoved to the side. The next thing she knew, she was lying on her back in the snow with Chase half over her.

The terrible screech of metal continued.

"Don't lift your head!" Chase shouted.

Eyes wide, protected from the wind by the snorkel hood, she watched in horror as the wing, lit from beneath by their flashlights slid over them, starting and stopping several times.

"Oh, my God," she whispered. "Oh, my God!"

The snow was so deep beneath her that she could have reached up and touched the wing as it jerked its way over her. Then, with a visible shudder, everything froze.

Chase's weight held her pinned in the snow, and she had no desire to move. Staring straight up at that wing, she waited for it to move again.

"We're going to crawl now," he said, leaning close to her ear. "Turn over, crawl straight under the wing."

For an instant after he levered off her, she wondered if she was going to be able to move at all. Then, with effort, hating to take her eyes off that potentially dangerous wing, she rolled over. Chase tugged her arm up the slope. Only at the last instant did she remember to grab her flashlight.

She hadn't realized how big that wing was. The journey beneath it, crab-crawling because she was afraid to lift herself, went on forever.

"Okay," Chase said. "Okay. You can sit up."

She did, twisting to look at the wing that now lay in the snow behind them, the front edge now nearly buried, the tunnels they had made crawling out rapidly filling.

"Everything's okay," Chase said, standing, his voice loud now to be heard over the wind. "Nothing's any worse. Maybe it's even better."

"Better?" Losing the last of her fear that somehow the weight of that wing was going to fall on her, she scrambled to her feet. "Better how?"

"The wing is buried at the front edge now. We'll get less movement."

Until the snow blew away. "How did that happen?"

"Apparently, when the plane slid forward, it tipped more."

"I don't know if that's good."

"Rory," he said, "at this minute I'm grabbing every straw."

He was right, she realized. There was no point in looking at negatives unless you could do something about them.

"We need to get back inside and reassure everyone. That slide must have worried them."

That was also true. She hoped it hadn't awakened Cait. Whether it had or not, those in the cabin must be wondering about whether more was coming and whether she and Chase were all right.

Once again they struggled into the wind and the upslope to round the rear of the plane. At moments like these, Rory appreciated just how big this jet was.

In her business she flew this way only as someone's guest. She preferred to be far more penurious with her travel expenses, and this kind of luxury had always struck her as unnecessary unless you had some kind of important work to do that you couldn't on a commercial flight—work that couldn't wait.

Cait couldn't wait, however, and she certainly couldn't travel by commercial airliner. Not in her weakened condition with her compromised immune system. This time, cost was the last thing Rory had considered.

But it was a huge plane.

When they reached the far side again, and the door, they discovered that the forward slippage had moved the plane so the door was blocked by deep snow.

"Hell," Chase said, then bent and started scooping snow with his hands.

Rory joined him. "You have everything else. How did you overlook a snow shovel?"

She thought she heard him snort, but the wind left her unsure.

"The best-laid plans," he quoted, scooping rapidly. "I think we may have lost our fire pit, too."

Rory glanced around, but as heavy as the snow was she doubted she could have made out the metal box. Why hadn't they thought to bring it inside? "We can make another one, right?"

"I hope. Mainly I hope we can get this door open. Then we'll worry about everything else."

She joined him in digging, growing hot inside her insulated clothing, but glad she no longer felt cold. She even started to perspire a bit and once again she noticed that she couldn't seem to get quite enough air.

"Stop." Chase reached out and gripped her arm. "You don't want to be breathing like that out here."

"Why not?"

"Altitude. And the air is extremely dry. You could get pulmonary edema."

"What about you?"

"I didn't come from sea level. This change isn't as big for me as it is for you."

She obeyed him, hating to feel useless, but his hands were big and strong, and even bigger inside gloves. Plus, the snow's dryness seemed to aid him, blowing away most of what he scooped to make a drift elsewhere.

"There," he said finally. The exit door was mostly unburied. He banged hard on it, and moments later they could hear banging from the inside. Yuma, and perhaps Wendy, were trying to shove the door open.

Chase worked his fingers into the crack on one side, and Rory immediately worked hers into the opening on the other side. Together they tugged, and at last the door began to swing down.

When they at last clambered inside, Rory threw back her hood but left her jacket on and unzipped. The cabin was warmer than outside, of course, but even though she had warmed up from her exertions, she could feel that it was still chilly inside. Perhaps too chilly.

She wanted to hurry back to Cait, but over the seats she could see her sister sitting up, holding a mug of something hot in her hands.

Cait's expression at once revealed that she had been terrified. "I was so scared for you," she said, her voice louder than Rory had heard it since coming home.

"We're fine," Rory assured her, easing past the others to reach her sister and sit beside her. "How are you doing?"

"I'm okay." Which was what Cait usually said.

"What happened?" Yuma asked.

Chase answered. "The plane slid forward about fifteen feet. Nothing seems to be any worse, though."

Wendy spoke. "We all just about panicked for you

two. Thank God you weren't right in front of this behemoth."

"We had to duck so the wing missed us, but it may have been a good thing. The leading edge is buried in the snow now. That'll help hold us in place."

"We tipped a little," Yuma remarked, "but not much. The really horrifying part was wondering about the two of you."

"Yeah," said Wendy an amused note in her voice. "The candles didn't even slide. We were fine in here."

"Thank God for that," Chase said.

Cait managed to lean forward and put her mug of broth on the table. Then she tugged her hand from beneath the blanket and reached out to grasp Rory's. "I'm glad you're okay," she murmured. Then her eyes fluttered closed, the last of her energy once again drained.

"Okay," Wendy announced. "The two of *you* go get some sleep. I think we're all going to be basically catnapping until we get out of here. I know I'm too wide awake to sleep now."

But Rory wasn't, she realized. The cold and the effort outside, plus the altitude made her wearier than she could remember being in a long time. Her eyelids seemed to be weighted in lead, and her limbs felt heavy. She could have slept right there. But even as she thought of lying down and sleeping, the desire for a bed grew even stronger. She gently drew her hand from Cait's slackened grip but hesitated, feeling guilty. Finally she gathered herself, needing to stretch out, needing the relative darkness, needing the comfort of a pillow to make sleep seem possible and right.

Odd, clinging to such a little notion in the midst of this mess. But God, she needed sleep or she was going to be worse than useless to her sister and everyone else.

At last she pushed herself to her feet and started to the back of the plane.

"Thanks for watching Cait," she said to Wendy.

"It's easy," Wendy assured her. "When I start to crash, I'll wake you, so don't worry."

"Thank you."

She doffed her jacket, snowpants and boots, this time keeping the felt boot liners on so her feet wouldn't get cold. It was definitely much chillier in the back of the plane than in the cabin, and she argued with herself for all of ten seconds about trying to sleep in the cabin before giving in to the lure of a very comfortable bed.

A short time after she stretched out on her side, she felt the blankets lift as Chase slipped in behind her, wrapping his arm around her waist.

"Warmth," he said.

She couldn't disagree. All of a sudden the small room didn't feel so cold, nor did she feel quite so alone.

"Thanks for saving me out there," she said.

"No problem. Not like I was going to stand by while that wing took off your head or broke your neck."

A little shiver ran through her as she remembered those moments. She had been so close to death or serious injury.

The shiver was misinterpreted. Chase immediately wrapped himself tighter around her and rubbed her arm gently.

"Sleep," he said. "God knows we're going to need clear heads before long."

Sleepy as she had been, now she felt wide awake to every nerve ending in her body. Her nipples had swollen, and each breath caused them to brush against the fabric of her bra, each time causing a pleasant tingle. She remained perfectly still, afraid of betraying how she felt, as syrupy desire steadily filled her. How was this possible? With all that was going on, how could she even be feeling this?

But the attempted guilt trip died as her body begged for more intimate touches, more intimate knowledge of the man who shared his warmth with her.

He shifted a little, and grew still.

Asleep? she wondered. But no, his breathing seemed more rapid, not the deep slow rhythms of sleep. Could he be feeling the same things? The same aching desire?

In spite of every voice in her head that screamed warnings, she wiggled a little back against him.

And felt it. Chase was as hard as a rock against her rear, as hungry for her as she was for him.

More objections popped up, thoughts about how she didn't know him, how her sister was in the next cabin at death's door, what a dangerous situation they were in. All the logical things that should be standing between her and these unwanted feelings.

But her body didn't agree. The desire that had begun to flame in her burned away all those rational objections, leaving her damp, hungry and needier than she could ever remember feeling.

And then it totally betrayed her, her hips arching back toward him.

She heard him catch his breath. He knew. She wanted to feel shame, but couldn't.

Then a shiver ripped through her as his hot lips found the nape of her neck, almost tentatively, in a soft kiss.

A whisper of breath escaped her, just a tiny bit—too quiet to be a moan. No sound. No sound, because there were people on the other side of an accordion door. Silence.

He kissed her again and she trembled.

She heard him whisper, "Oh, hell, you're going to hate me."

At that moment she couldn't believe it would ever be possible to hate Chase Dakota, unless he pulled away right then.

But he didn't pull away. His lips trailed to her ear, and she felt his hot breath in her ear. She shivered again and this time clasped his hand, holding onto it for dear life, giving consent. Maybe even begging.

"You are so sexy," he whispered in her ear, his breath causing her to shiver with longing again. "So sexy."

That was the last thing either of them said.

His hand tugged free of hers, slipping up beneath layers of clothing to find her naked breast, already aching for his touch. He brushed his thumb over her nipple, driving her insane with need, causing her to feel damp between her legs.

Over and over he teased that nipple, causing shocks of pleasure to tear through her as if on wings. His lips left moist patches on her neck, on her cheeks that grew cold as soon as he moved on. The contrast excited her even more.

Slowly, her hips pressed back against him, feeling his stiffness, thrilled by it. Little by little she began to rock in the rhythm of love, not caring how or when, knowing only that she was helpless to stop this now. The longing he evoked left her mindless.

She retained only enough sense to hold back her moans, and it wasn't easy. She wasn't a normally noisy lover, but he made her want to cry out over and over.

Then suddenly his hand slipped downward. He didn't even unfasten her pants. He cupped her hard, almost forcing a groan from her. She rocked into that pressure, needing it and more. Then his hips met the rhythm of hers, pressing into her bottom in time with the squeezing, rubbing motion of his hand.

She felt surrounded by desire, claimed as she'd never been claimed before. Aching, needing, helpless, trapped between his hands and his hips in deepening desire.

A slave to the feelings he awoke in her, and glad to be right there, right then.

His ministrations continued, somehow unbearably sexy, sexier than if he'd stripped the clothes from her body. It felt deliciously illicit, and her hunger discovered new heights.

Squeezing and rubbing, pressing himself against her from the other side, he created a rope of passion that bound her to him as tightly as if he had entered her.

At the very pinnacle, she thought she would shatter. She had to bite her lip to keep herself from screaming, literally.

As clenching waves of satisfaction ripped through her, she felt him stiffen, then shudder. He had found his completion, too.

Chapter 6

He never took his hand away from her, but continued to hold her tightly, making her feel claimed and oddly safe. As sleep fought to take her, she found it easier to let it. He had drained all the tension from her, leaving her soft, tired and so relaxed.

When she awoke, Chase was rolling away from her.

"Wendy says she's having trouble keeping her eyes open."

At once Rory sprang to her feet. She felt the need to wash, to change, but even changing into something from her carry-on needed to wait. Cait first.

Chase was out of the bedroom almost before her feet hit the floor. She smiled rather grimly. He probably wanted a postmortem about as much as she did, which was to say not at all.

Their unorthodox sex needed to be confined to some dustbin at the back of their memories for many good reasons. If the memory of those moments wouldn't leave her alone, then she'd remind herself of every single one of them.

It had been good, it had probably been born of adrenaline, their unusual circumstances and some crazy need to affirm life in the face of all the danger they faced. Better to forget it than dwell on it.

Maybe someday, when she was an old lady, she could drag the memory out and remember the brief period when she'd tossed out every inhibition to be with a stranger. Old ladies could safely indulge those memories, and maybe even cackle over them with glee. If she looked too closely at it right now, she might wonder if she had lost her mind.

Well, she had, she thought as she slipped her jacket and boots on again, then headed up front to Cait. She'd gone nuts for fifteen or twenty glorious minutes, if that long.

It was okay to go nuts sometimes. It happened. Over the last few weeks, plenty had been pushing her in that direction.

Cait was still sleeping, but a touch found her cheek warm, and her breathing seemed regular, if a bit shallow.

"I got her to cough some more," Wendy said. "And she had another cup of sweet tea. She seems fine right now."

Fine. Not exactly the word Rory would apply, but she understood Wendy's meaning. "Thank you."

Wendy squeezed her arm, then disappeared into the bedroom with her husband.

"This is a fractured night," Chase remarked. He glanced at his watch. "Close to endless, too. Coffee? Soup?"

"Coffee." She straightened and started to follow him to the galley, but he waved her back.

"Sit with your sister. I can make coffee."

He also probably didn't want to be too close to her. That might be a good idea right now. Pretend it didn't happen, and don't give either of them a chance to talk about it. Sometimes silence was wise, and Rory felt this was one of them.

But wise or not, she couldn't help remembering. Judging by her response to the memory, her body wanted a rerun even if her mind warned her it would be dangerous and maybe even stupid. Even with her sister sleeping right beside her. God, was she losing her mind?

It was as if this crash and her sister's illness had unleashed a whole bunch of stuff inside her that she'd been keeping under for too long. The side of Aurora Campbell that she never let anyone see: the woman.

Twenty minutes later Chase returned with steaming mugs and put one on the table in front of her. Then he sat across from her and Cait. Some part of her was surprised that he hadn't sought the solitude of the cockpit.

But he didn't seem to be avoiding her, and that made her feel a bit better. Damn, she was a tangle of emotions right now, acting in a way she wouldn't ordinarily act, having feelings that seemed to come out of nowhere and didn't resemble anything remotely logical.

Why would she have felt bad if he had avoided her? Wasn't that basically what she was advocating by trying to pretend that nothing had happened?

She sighed quietly and sipped her coffee, looking again at Cait. No, she couldn't do a damn thing for her sister right now except sit here and worry. What good was that? So she turned back to Chase.

"Do you have enough insurance to get another plane?"

"Of course. I'm covered for everything. But I doubt I'm going to need it. We had a mechanical failure on the first flight after a major overhaul."

She nodded. "But you're out of business for a while."

"Yeah, but I can make it. What's going to tick me off is losing regular customers unless I can rent something in the meantime."

"That would be tough. Believe me, I know."

"Are you losing customers right now?" he asked bluntly.

"Not yet. But it could happen if I don't get back on the job soon enough. For the moment my clients are understanding." That was something she refused to worry about right now. At this moment in time, Cait was unquestionably more important than a mere business. Even though it had taken her years to build.

"They should be. Some things come before business."

"Not always."

"No," he agreed. He sipped his coffee and put his mug on the table.

She tried another tack. "So what's the likelihood that the storm is interfering with the GPS?"

"I can't give you percentages. All radio transmissions can be disrupted by atmospheric conditions, and the GPS is trying to reach a satellite. That's usually more reliable than other line-of-sight methods, which is why I have it, but things can affect it. Ionization in the upper atmosphere, for example. For all I know the aurora is active right now. Then there's the moisture in the air column. This is a really bad storm, which means lots of moisture at the upper levels, so that could be interrupting the signal. When it starts to pass, we'll know for sure."

She looked at the table in front of her. "I'm not good at being helpless."

"Me, neither. But that's where we are until later today or early tomorrow. I don't want to muck around with wiring too much until I'm sure it's not just the storm. I might break something that isn't broken."

A quiet, humorless laugh escaped her. "I second that."

He was silent for a minute then said, "You shouldn't feel so guilty. It's not your fault that your sister is sick, and you're doing everything you can."

She felt a spark of anger. "That doesn't help."

"I know it doesn't. Chalk it to something I just needed to say. Cait's lucky to have you. Too many people have no one at all."

There was no argument against that. She had tightened her lips, but now she let them relax. What was the point? Life was what it was, and sometimes it was a bitch.

Then she caught a possible subtext in what he had said. "Do you have someone?"

"I have friends. No family. Only child."

"Your parents?"

He nodded. "My dad was a pilot, too. Unfortunately, he had a small single-engine plane of his own. Well, I guess I shouldn't say *unfortunately*. He got a lot of pleasure out of it. But two years after I graduated from the academy, they took a trip in Alaska and went down in the mountains."

"I'm very sorry." It struck her that the current situation must be reminding him of that, stirring all kinds of emotional echoes for him. But she didn't know how to broach the subject. What right did she have to pry? A brief experience of sex didn't make them any less strangers.

He looked around the nearly dark cabin. "We were damn lucky," he said.

"We had a bigger plane and apparently an outstanding pilot."

"Size *does* make a difference," he said. Then he startled her by winking.

"You didn't just say that!" She had to bite back the most unexpected giggle.

He cocked a brow. "The air was getting heavy. The situation is heavy enough."

"No denying that," she agreed. Amazing how he had just lightened her mood. Then he surprised her again by leaning over and opening a small drawer under the table. He tossed a pack of cards between them. "Name your poison."

How many hours had she spent in oil fields playing cards with her coworkers? More than she could count. She reached for the pack, opened it and pulled the jokers out of the deck. "Seven-card stud," she said.

He had some poker chips, too, and soon they were deep in the game. A good form of distraction, and an equally good excuse not to get personal.

She just wished she knew whether to be grateful for that or not.

"So," she said, "tell me about Wendy and Billy Joe." That seemed safe enough. "Wendy told me a little. They're an interesting pair."

"More interesting than most of us realize. I was young at the time they got together, and too busy with other things to really pay attention to the rumor mill. It did create a stir because he was so much older and folks pretty much had him figured as a permanent loner."

"Because of his PTSD?"

"Partly, I guess. Like I said, it wasn't really on my radar. But I got the impression that our old sheriff, Wendy's dad, was on the horns of a real dilemma."

"How so?"

"Yuma was his friend, and Wendy was his daughter, and he didn't want either of them getting hurt." He chuckled quietly. "From what I know of her dad, he probably warned them both off the other. He's never been a man to mince his words if his dander gets up, and I bet his dander was up about this one."

"But age isn't necessarily a determining factor."

"Most of the time I'd agree. But you can imagine where he was coming from. Yuma was a vet with some issues, and Wendy was his little girl. He probably saw disaster written all over it for both of them."

"Evidently he would have been wrong."

"Evidently. They've been married a long time now." He smiled, his eyes crinkling. "Your deal."

Chase was finding it hard to accept that just a few hours ago he had acted like a randy teenager in the back of a car with Rory. The intensity of wanting her had overwhelmed him, especially when he had sensed that she might be feeling the same way.

He wanted to put it all down to their situation—if anyone knew how danger could heighten the sex drive, it was him—but he couldn't quite.

Rory wasn't just a stranger to him, even though they hadn't known each other twenty-four hours yet. Situations like this compressed emotional time, and you got to know important things about people when so much

was on the line. However, he warned himself to be careful because she was going to be flying on to Minnesota
with her sister, then back to Mexico.

A rueful thought struck him: Maybe all his girlfriend
problems over the years had stemmed from his own
choices. Maybe, at some level, he kept picking women
he knew wouldn't stick.

He'd certainly picked one here.

But having watched Rory with her sister, he knew
that while circumstance would carry her away from
him, she was at heart a "sticker." Once she cared about
someone, apparently there was no limit to her caring.
Yes, people loved their families, but they also had
limits. Cait was dying. He was sure insurance wasn't
going to pay for this experimental treatment; it never
did. And the cost of hiring him and his plane for this
trip was exorbitant.

A lot of loving people, looking at this prognosis,
and hearing that their loved one just wanted to give
up, would, with great grief, give in. They would listen
to doctors who said it was impossible to save Cait,
to doctors who had evidently said Cait was in such a
condition the treatment, already uncertain, probably
wouldn't work. But here was a woman who was risking her career, spending a fortune, probably planning
to pay for uncovered treatments that would leave her
in debt for a long time to come…because she loved her
sister.

That didn't make Rory one-of-a-kind, but it sure
made her relatively rare in his experience.

They'd been playing in silence for about a half hour
when he had to ask the question. "Did you have to fight
to get Cait into this experimental treatment?"

She looked up, her face tightening. "Like a pit bull," she said finally.

"I wondered."

"You were right to wonder. She might skew their results because she's so weak, and that could affect the drug's evaluation."

"So how did you manage it?"

"I argued my way up the chain until I got to the guys who designed the drug and were having it tested. I managed to convince them that it would help them a whole lot if they got a good outcome with someone so far along. More than it would by only picking people who'd just gotten sick. And then I argued that they could quite easily list her as an outlier because of her condition, and use that as an excuse for removing her from their evaluation if it doesn't work."

One corner of his mouth lifted. "You really don't give up."

"Giving up has never gotten me anywhere. I might not be able to make it, when all is said and done, but if you give up, you never find out, do you?"

"Absolutely not." The quiet admiration he'd begun to feel for her despite his initial irritation at her pushiness, grew. "You know, I hope if I ever need someone in my corner, I get someone like you."

Thanks to the candle he had placed on the table so they could read the cards, he was able to see her blush. My God, Rory could blush. That tickled him somehow. He would have thought her long past it.

"Just doing what needs doing," she said quietly.

Exactly what most heroic people said, he thought. He was tempted to say so, but figured he'd embarrassed her enough.

She pushed her cards aside. "Enough of that."

"Sure." He started scooping them up into a neat pile. "Maybe more later."

He nodded, sensing that her mind had wandered off somewhere. Probably to the hours, perhaps days, ahead. He was with her in worry right now. But he could hardly tell her how furious and sickened he would feel if Cait were lost while in his care.

Because she *was* in his care. He was captain of this crashed ship, and her life was in his hands as surely as if he were one of her doctors. He had to get her out of here before her medicine ran out, before she came down with something else in her weakened state.

Nor was he the kind of man who could just shrug it off and say it wasn't his fault the plane crashed and that Cait was so ill.

No, he wasn't made that way. It was killing him that at the moment he could do so little to protect his passengers, especially Cait. He knew they could hang out for weeks in this plane. He had enough food, enough candles, and with the snow there'd be plenty of water. But none of that would help Cait if her drugs ran out. Four days. By the time the storm blew through, they'd be down to two. If the beacon wasn't working...

He didn't want to think about that. Sitting here waiting for rescue without a beacon, in a plane that would be invisible under the snow, might cost them Cait. So if they didn't get GPS back, how long could he afford to spend trying to fix things before they'd have to try to hike out, because waiting would ensure Cait's death?

He didn't like their odds.

He leaned back, closing his eyes for a moment. Cusswords floated through his mind, but they didn't help at all, especially since he held them in. A little swearing might ease his anger at this situation, but doing it silently inside his head just fueled his rage.

Some freaking mechanic somewhere was going to pay for this.

He looked at Rory. "People make mistakes."

"Yes, they do." Her look questioned him.

"But some people, given what rides on what they do, shouldn't make them."

"I agree. But, unfortunately, they do anyway. Even brain surgeons."

"I know."

"The point is?"

"Right now I'd like to strangle a mechanic."

"Ah." One corner of her mouth lifted. "I felt that way just recently about some roughnecks."

"I'm sure you did. I'm just really angry right now."

"So vent. I'm angry, too. I was going to be angry with you, until you explained what happened. I'll join you in thinking of horrible ways to deal with that mechanic, whoever he is."

"It had to be mechanical failure." He'd run over this in his mind a thousand times since the crash, but for some reason he needed to run over it again. "Something caused us to lose fuel fast—faster than a simple leak. And I can't think of anything except that something was wired poorly—or loose—something that caused us to just dump the fuel. It happened that fast, and I couldn't stop it."

She nodded. "Kinda like I felt when I realized those guys hadn't stopped drilling."

"Yeah." He shook his head, all of a sudden back in the cockpit in those minutes leading up to disaster. "Fuel jettison equipment was optional on this plane."

"You mean they don't all have it?"

"No. It depends on the structure. Some planes don't have to lighten their loads to land safely. This one had it as an option, and obviously I didn't buy it new. But I thought it was an advantage."

"Why?"

"Because the last thing you want in a crash is a lot of aviation fuel onboard. So I just felt it was better to have a plane with a jettison system than one without. Never occurred to me it might *cause* a crash."

"Do you suppose because it was optional somebody didn't check it out?"

"I don't know. I guess the NTSB will find out. If that's what happened. I'm just guessing that's the cause, but I suppose something else could have gone wrong."

"The more complex the equipment…" She let the thought dangle. He certainly didn't need her to finish it.

He closed his eyes again, envisioning the gauges as the whole flight went to hell. By the time he was sure what was happening and that he couldn't stop it, they were in deep trouble. That fast.

"Reliving it won't help," she said quietly.

His eyes snapped open. "You read minds?"

"Sometimes. No, it's just that I know. I replayed my orders to those roughnecks a thousand times. I wrote down my exact words and had a native Spanish speaker look them over. I hadn't misspoken in either language. Then I moved on to wondering what else I could have done."

"I'll get there, I suppose."

"Maybe not. You got us down in one piece. I don't know a whole lot about planes, but when the engines flamed out, a lot of other equipment probably stopped working, too."

"It did. And when I replace this plane, I'm getting one with a windmill, to generate power if the engines fail. We have some auxiliary power, but it's not a lot and it doesn't work for long. Shortly after the flame-out, I started to lose my hydraulic pumps. Mechanics alone weren't enough. The aux drains fast."

"I thought so. From my narrow knowledge base, I assumed most of the power was coming from the turbines."

"It does, because that's efficient. The engines do two jobs. If you think about it, it makes perfect sense. When do I need aux power? Just for the length of time it takes to board and get the engines going. Or long enough to run emergency lighting for evacuation. Why carry another generator?"

"I agree."

He shook his head, tired of his own internal hamster wheel. "The odds against this were incredible. No amount of planning would have conceived of this."

"Unlike my well disaster."

"Point taken."

She smiled faintly. "I wasn't trying to make any point. That was agreement."

He liked being able to talk to her, he realized. She understood what fascinated him in ways most people didn't. She might not be intimately acquainted with planes, but she could discuss aviation intelligently and she didn't give him the feeling that she was hiding boredom.

Another sign that he'd been selecting all the wrong women. "So flying is my life, and oil is yours."

She nodded. "For now. Someday I hope to have things built up enough that I can delegate more, maybe spend less time in the field. I actually feel pretty root-less now."

"At least I have a home base. Do you?"

She shook her head. "I don't keep an apartment or anything. My office is my computer and my cell phone. Soon I hope to be a little beyond that. With a real office. And not needing to be in the field quite so much."

She averted her gaze briefly. "I wasn't thinking about the really important issues. This situation has made me reconsider. A career isn't everything. I haven't even been good about visiting Cait. I just assumed she was happy with Hal and didn't need me."

"How could you know if she didn't tell you?"

"I know, but I still feel guilty. You take some things for granted until life rears up and reminds you that you might lose them."

"I think we all do that."

"I'm sure. But it doesn't make it right." She gave an-other little shake of her head, looked at her sister and then at him again. "I've been questioning myself a lot the last couple of weeks. About what's essential, and where I really want to be in ten or twenty years. Cait had the life she wanted all laid out in front of her, and now look. So what's life about, Chase? Have you ever figured that one out?"

He shifted a little, feeling a bit awkward. He wasn't used to discussions like this, at least not since his youth when cosmic questions had been hot topics. At twenty you thought of them, and believed you might figure them out. Then you got older and got way too busy to even wonder.

Yet what better time than now, stranded on a moun-tainside in a blizzard, in the company of a very sick woman? He could well understand why Rory was wondering, and if he were honest with himself, he probably should be wondering, too.

"I haven't been thinking about it," he admitted. "Flying is—was—my whole life. I expend most of my efforts to keep myself in the air. To grow my business enough that I don't have costly downtime. But…that's not enough, is it?"

"Are you asking me?"

"I'm asking myself, but I'll listen to answers."

"It's not enough," she said firmly. "It's not that I haven't been living, but I've been living with such an intense, single-minded focus. Cait's illness has forced me to think about the parts of life I've been neglecting. I'm not sure yet which ones I want, but one thing I'm fairly certain of is that my life is going to broaden after this. I can't be consumed with work and business, however adventurous it may seem."

"A lot of people would think you live a broad life already. Travel, other cultures, that sort of thing."

"But it's all about work. I don't put down roots—all my friends are in the business. I've been asking myself what I'll have left when that's gone. Not much."

"I know. I haven't been thinking about it, but you're making me." He felt emotions beginning to roil inside him, emotions he couldn't quite identify. It was as if he sensed a big change coming, but didn't know what it might be or if he would like it.

And for the last day, since the crash, he'd been looking at Wendy and Yuma. They were so close they seemed to communicate without words, to find comfort in each other's presence. To be a self-sustaining unit even in the midst of crisis. If he allowed himself to be honest, didn't he want the same kind of relationship? Eventually?

"It's easy," Rory said, "to push matters down the road. To tell yourself you'll get to it later. Well, time is passing, and how can I be sure there'll be a later?"

"Obvious question right now," he admitted.

Her gaze grew intense. "Let's be honest," she said. "We can't be sure we'll get out of this mess. There's no guarantee. Not just for Cait, but for any of us."

He didn't argue, because even though he believed they could make it, with the possible exception of Cait, the fact remained that he hadn't planned on a plane crash, either. What if he hadn't been able to bring them down in one piece?

"I don't think I'd like my own epitaph," he admitted. "What's it going to say? *He flew?*"

"Yeah. Mine wouldn't be much different. It's going to be an empty tombstone if I don't make some changes."

"Do you have any in mind?"

"I don't know," she said. "Cait wanted to have a family. She couldn't and they didn't discover why until they diagnosed her illness."

"You want a family?"

"I've begun thinking about it. I mean, what does it come down to, Chase? What is our legacy going to be? If we die in the next few days, what will it all have meant?"

"I don't know." But she was sure making him think about it. "You're right. It's easy to just push stuff down the road. And some of them…well, it's not as if you can just make them happen."

"True," she admitted. "Having a family means finding the right person to do it with. But there are other things. Other legacies. Other reasons for people to say I didn't just take up space. Kids aren't the only one."

"No. But maybe the one that matters is love. And if

that's the case, you're doing a damn fine job of it with your sister."

In the flickering candlelight, he saw her mouth curve into a faint smile. "Love? A man mentions love?"

Now he really *did* feel awkward. "Why not? You want to talk about the meaning of life and what matters, well, even a stupid guy like me can figure out that what matters is the lives you touch, and how you touch them."

"I'm sorry," she said instantly. "I guess I'm a little down on men at the moment. Cait's husband."

"And those guys who didn't listen to you about not drilling." But he appreciated her apology anyway. At least she wasn't the kind of woman who hated all men on principle. If he was going to be disliked, he wanted it to be for something he'd done. There's been ample reason in his life for that. Wasn't there for everyone? But a sense of discomfort began to niggle at him.

"I work with men all the time," she went on. "Most of the time, in fact. I really don't have anything against men in general. I don't know why that popped out."

"I do," he said with a quiet laugh. "Most guys *do* run like scared rabbits at the mention of love."

Her smile widened. "You're not talking about only that kind of love anyway."

"No, I'm not." Unaccustomed as he was to this kind of discussion, he found himself reluctant to drop it. The quiet intimacy growing between them in the near dark was satisfying something in him, just as their earlier sex had satisfied a need. Only this one seemed so much more profound.

So he looked for a way to continue it. "Yuma," he said finally.

"What about him?"

"He tried to walk away from life," Chase said thoughtfully.

"Wendy said something about that."

"Yeah, for years he lived in these mountains with a bunch of Vietnam vets who couldn't handle the rest of the world. I don't know a whole lot about post-traumatic stress disorder, but I guess if you live among triggers, it can get pretty bad."

"That's what I hear."

"So he hid for a while. Then he came down out of the mountains and started flying our medevac helicopter. The same kind of helicopter he'd flown in Vietnam."

"I can only imagine how hard that must have been," Rory observed.

"Me, too. Anyway, he never forgot the rest of the guys in the mountains. And every working day he does something important for really sick people. Long after he's gone, people in Conard County are going to remember him."

"Not everybody can have that kind of impact, though," Rory noted.

"No, but right now I'm flying tycoons around. It's a job that pays me to do what I love. That's not a legacy. That's a toy."

"Whoa!" She looked shocked. "Don't put yourself down like that. You said you had friends. Maybe you do a lot for them and don't even realize it."

"I don't know," he said ruefully.

"Man!" It almost sounded like a curse. "So what should I say? I run around finding oil for tycoons? Ouch."

"I didn't say anything about you."

"You didn't have to. The thing is, you're right. Obviously, we both do something that people are willing to pay us to do, but if that's all we do…" She trailed off, frowning.

Chase felt annoyed with himself. His own self-examination hadn't been intended to put her down, but he'd done just that.

As he began to wonder if she'd ever say another word to him, she spoke. "Clearly, at least I need to do something in addition to work. Just more food for thought."

At least she wasn't angry at him, but he was a bit angry at himself. He seemed to be finding maturity late, propelled by this woman's devotion to her sister. Things to which he hadn't given much thought gnawed at him now. He wasn't that old—thirty-six—but he ought to realize by now that in a few eyeblinks he'd wake up some morning and realize that he was forty. Then fifty. He was no longer the young turk who had graduated from the academy and leapt into a career of flying high-performance jets. If failing his flight physical hadn't gotten that through to him in an enduring way, this certainly had.

He'd merely transferred his passion, but he hadn't improved himself. Maybe this whole airline business of his was the emotional equivalent of a pacifier. Still flying, still busy and still very much the jock aviator.

"Damn," he said.

"What?"

"I guess I still have a lot of growing up to do."

She smiled, giving a quiet laugh. "I think we spend our entire lives trying to grow up. But I'm sure reevaluating."

He was, too. And, oddly, he felt more comfortable with it now. Maybe because they'd talked about it.

They fell silent then, Cait slumbering between them

almost like a human signpost, pointing out all the things he'd been ignoring. And maybe Rory, too.

He watched her fall into her own thoughts, and noted yet again how pretty she was, how very attractive. Her devotion to her sister only enhanced her magnetism.

He looked at the two women and finally admitted that there was a huge hole in his life. A crater, actually. One he hadn't even noticed before.

Chapter 7

Morning arrived at last. Rory had dozed fitfully in the seat beside her sister, waking at every little sound. She'd been aware of people moving around from time to time, of the exit door opening a little, briefly, to let in fresh air.

Then the sound of Cait's breathing caught her attention. She sat bolt upright and listened, seeing Chase in the seat across from her.

She knew it was morning only because he'd raised the window shade beside him, and faint light filtered in.

She turned her attention to Cait and heard him say, "I was just thinking about waking you. Her breathing changed just a few minutes ago."

Cait's breaths were shallow, but they rattled a bit, too. Rory felt the sting of panic.

"I'll get Wendy," Chase said.

Rory nodded, leaning over to wake Cait.

"Cait? Cait, sweetie, wake up. Please."

It took several attempts, but Cait's eyes at last opened. "I'm so tired," she whispered.

"I know, Cait. I know. Do you think you can cough?"

Cait tried but the effort was weak.

Then Wendy appeared, looking tousled but fully awake. She listened to Cait's chest with her ear, and Rory caught the look in her eyes, though it was quickly concealed. Wendy was worried.

"Okay," Wendy said. "We've got to humidify this air. Chase, more candles. Rory, get that thing you made for boiling water. I want it here on the table. And Chase, can you find anything I can use to tent her so she'll get the moisture?"

"I've got survival blankets."

"That'll do."

All of a sudden the plane was a beehive of activity. Yuma appeared, too, and as soon as they had the chafing dish heating in front of Cait, he and Chase announced that they were going out to build a fire and make some kind of breakfast.

Rory lifted the window blind beside her, and in the weak light outside could tell only that the blizzard was still raging. Hard to believe that they'd left Seattle less than a day ago. It felt like a lifetime.

When the plane's door opened, a blast of arctic air blew in, bringing a cloud of fine snow with it. Rory looked out again after they closed the door and saw the men disappear into the maelstrom of snow. Build a fire in this?

But that problem couldn't engage her attention. Cait was all she could think about. She helped Wendy spread a mylar blanket to make a tent to make sure Cait got all the steam from the water that had just begun to boil. She slipped under the tent with her sister to keep an eye on her.

"I'll get stuff together and make her a hot drink in the galley," Wendy said.

"Thanks." Rory found her sister's hand and held it. To her horror, it didn't feel cool. Too warm? She touched Cait's cheek gently and was mildly reassured to find that it wasn't hot. Not feverish. Not yet.

In their little cocoon, light from the candle reflected off the mylar and made it almost bright. Cait struggled back to wakefulness.

"Breathe, sweetie," Rory urged her sister. "The steam will help."

Cait surprised her with the shadow of a smile. "At least it's warm."

"Yeah. It is." The mylar was helping with that, too. "Wendy's making you something hot to drink. And you need to take your meds again, too."

One solitary tear rolled down Cait's cheek. "I'm sorry, Rory. I'm messing up your life."

"Don't be sorry. Whatever you do, don't apologize to me. I wish I could do more, not less."

"I'm lucky you're my sister."

Rory forced a smile. "I'm glad you're my sister, too."

Cait gave a little laugh, but it barely started to emerge before it vanished in a deep, barking cough.

"That's good," Wendy's voice said from outside the tent. "Get her to lean forward. I'm going to tap her back."

Tap? Rory thought. The way Wendy did it, it was more than a tap. But essential, too. Absolutely essential.

She wrapped her arm around Cait's front and bent

her forward, making sure she didn't get too close to the hot water and the candle. Then, Wendy pounded Cait's back.

After several tries, Cait coughed again. It still sounded tight, but at least a little seemed to loosen.

"Five more minutes," Wendy said. "Then we'll try again."

"I'm sorry I'm so tired," Cait whispered.

"Don't think about it. We're going to get you to that hospital, and on that new drug. You're going to get better." Maybe she was a fool, but she couldn't allow herself to consider anything else.

"I almost believe you," Cait sighed.

That was an improvement, Rory thought. Small but significant. Will to live, she believed, was as important as any pill or IV, and her greatest source of concern the last few weeks had been Cait's apparent desire to just give up.

It took a half hour, but they managed to loosen Cait's chest enough that her breathing sounded better. And after all that, she still had enough strength to drink some soup and take her pills.

Wendy had removed the tent, setting it aside, saying they'd use it again in a couple of hours. But she didn't take the chafing dish away. She added more water to it, humidifying the entire plane.

"It's hell out there" was Chase's pronouncement as he and Yuma finally returned to the cabin, having successfully managed to throw together a meal, a stew made of whatever foods they had onboard that they thought would go together reasonably well.

To Rory it tasted like ambrosia. It didn't matter what was in it, only that it was full of calories. They finished off with hot coffee, and even though she liked her coffee black, she added sugar for fuel.

They huddled close while they ate, and lit more candles for warmth. Under other circumstances it would have felt cozy.

But Rory's mental clock was ticking loudly again. Three more days of medicine for her sister, and now breathing problems for which they had no treatment but a jerry-rigged humidifier. The fear she had been feeling since she learned of her sister's illness ramped up again, agitating her, making it almost impossible for her to hold still.

But there wasn't a damn thing she could do.

"Maybe when this storm clears," Yuma said, "I can figure out where we are. I used to walk all over these mountains. I might recognize a landmark."

"That would help," Chase said. "Especially if I can get the radio to work. Then it won't matter so much if the GPS doesn't come back up."

Rory perked up a bit, feeling a ray of hope. "You mean we could find our own way out of here?"

"That'll depend," Yuma said.

"Well, obviously. It's just good to know there might be an option other than hoping the beacon works, and works soon enough."

"Not a great option," Chase warned her. "Getting down these mountains through fresh snowfall will be challenging."

Rory glanced over at Cait, sending a clear message. Cait's condition made it impossible for them to wait. The clock just kept ticking. In fact, it seemed to be accelerating, especially with Cait's new breathing problem.

But she knew now that everyone on this plane

cared about getting Cait out of here alive. If this had to happen, she couldn't have asked for a better group of companions.

After breakfast they tented Cait again while the guys went out to wash dishes over the fire in the snow. It was still blowing so hard that when Rory glanced out, she could barely see them, and the fire looked dim.

Another fifteen minutes of steam, and Cait began to cough hard. Rory felt another prick of fear, because there was no ignoring the fact that Cait was coughing way too much to be explained away simply by her being so exhausted and not breathing deeply enough.

Again she caught that look of concern in Wendy's gaze. Cait had no resistance left and was taking drugs that suppressed her immune system. If she was developing pneumonia, it would hit her fast and hard. Maybe too fast to get her out of here.

But Wendy laid her hand on Cait's forehead, then nodded. "No fever."

"But this congestion could cause serious problems, right?"

"If we don't keep on top of it. We'll keep at it, though. I promise."

Cait had fallen back to sleep as soon as she cleared her lungs, and apparently didn't hear their concern. Good. Rory figured her sister didn't need another complication, most especially another reason to give up hope. She feared Cait would do exactly that, too, after what she'd seen in her these past few weeks. Never in her worst imaginings had she thought Cait would just want to give up. It seemed so unlike the Cait she used to be, and was probably the best indicator of just how bad Cait felt.

Rory could hardly stand to think about it. Never had

she reached a point in her life where she might have wanted to die, but when she imagined how her sister must be feeling to want to give up this way, the pain became almost unendurable.

"We've got to get her to drink more," Wendy went on. "It's essential. Lots of sweet tea and soup. As much as we can get into her. She needs the calories and she needs the fluids to keep her chest loose. Every half hour if we can."

Rory nodded, adding another ticking clock to the one at the back of her mind. "I'll keep on it."

"We both will."

Time might be running out even faster than she had thought. She wasn't much of a praying woman, but lately she'd been praying a lot. Now she added another prayer, begging God for mercy for her sister.

Chase disappeared into the cockpit again, determined to see what he could do with the GPS and radio communication. He emerged a long time later, looking grim. In answer to their questioning looks, he shrugged.

"Nothing."

But the storm was still blowing heavily, rescue was out of the question until it passed, and maybe that was the only thing wrong with their communications. They couldn't be sure until the storm subsided.

That was an uncertainty she had to live with, like it or not. She loathed it.

"I think," Chase said, "that we need to take alternating naps throughout the day. None of us got enough sleep last night, and tonight we'll still have to keep watch." He paused. "From what I recall of this storm system, it should clear out sometime late tonight or early tomorrow morning. We need to be rested and ready to deal with whatever we have to do."

Rory didn't think she could sleep, so Wendy and Yuma agreed to take the first nap. Chase sat across from her again, and Rory noticed that he looked at Cait with real concern.

"We'll get her out of here," he said yet again. "One way or another if I have to carry her down this mountain on my back."

It didn't sound like bravado, but rather like real determination. Rory felt a rush of warmth toward him.

"I'm scared," she admitted, not an easy thing for her to do. Admitting mistakes was one thing; admitting fear entirely another. In her life she had to always keep her fear hidden, because there was a danger the men she worked with would see it as weakness. As a result, she'd come to see it as weakness, too. But she could no longer pretend it didn't exist. She was terrified of losing Cait.

His gray eyes settled on her. "Only a fool wouldn't be scared right now, and your sister's situation only makes it worse. But we'll get her out of here."

"You can't really promise that." Her voice broke, and she realized with horror that she was on the verge of tears. "Oh, God," she said quietly, her voice thickening. "I can't break down."

"Why not? Sometimes it helps. Cry if you need to. God knows, you've got plenty of reasons."

"I'm so worried."

He nodded. "I don't like that coughing, either. I'll help when you need to tent her again."

"Thanks."

He startled her by reaching across the table and clasping her hand. The warmth and contact felt good, so she turned hers over so they were palm to palm. He squeezed gently.

"Last night," he started to say.

She cut him off. "We don't have to discuss it. It happened."

He frowned. "Was it that bad?"

Her head jerked backward in surprise. "I didn't say that."

A slow, sexy smile came to his face. "Ah."

She felt her cheeks heat. "Chase, please. I don't know what came over me."

"I do. *I* did." His smile widened a shade. "Do you hate me for it?"

"Of course not!"

"Well, then. I wanted to hate myself for it, but I enjoyed it too much. You really are one sexy woman."

She gaped at him, then glanced quickly at Cait. Her sister still slept. "Me?" she said finally, quietly. "Not me. And certainly not now. I haven't showered since yesterday morning, I haven't changed my clothes, I feel like something that ought to be in the dustbin."

"Funny, that isn't turning me off at all."

She told herself he was just trying to distract her from her worries, and maybe he was. But no, the glint in his eyes said he meant every word.

"I just thought," he continued, "that since I took advantage of you last night instead of just keeping you warm, I ought to be a gentleman and tell you it was wonderful. And not at all meaningless."

"How could it mean anything? You don't know me." But she liked the part about it being wonderful. A trickle of warmth wended its way to her center.

"It meant something. I'm thirty-six years old, Rory.

I don't do that with just anyone. And I figured you had a right to know that. I'm not sixteen anymore."

Her cheeks grew hotter. Mainly because she was basically inexperienced with this kind of conversation. Only once since college had she made love with a man because she spent all her time making sure her conduct was professional and that nothing she did would make any man perceive her as a sexual being. That was particularly important in the places where she worked. Gossip could grow fast, and undermine her authority.

"As for not knowing you," he continued quietly, "I think you're wrong. I don't know all your historical details, but I've had the opportunity to watch you under tremendous pressure. Times like these show our real character, believe me."

He had a point, she admitted. In these conditions you either stepped up or you fell down. A lot could be learned.

In fact, thinking about it, she realized that she knew the truly important things about Chase now. Not just that he was a great pilot, but that he took care of the people in his charge. He was strong, determined and even kind.

Kind enough to promise to get Cait out of here if he had to carry her on his back. The kind of man you'd want at your side in hard times. That said a lot.

"Anyway," he said, "I just wanted you to know. Last night happened because you, not anybody else, make me hot enough to forget the niceties. No roses, no dinner, no champagne. Shoot, that'll have to wait for another day. In fact, I'm going to ask you right now for a date."

"A date?" She almost could have laughed, given their

circumstances, but she knew it would probably sound bitter.

"A date. The first one won't be much, sorry to say. But the second one, after we get out of here and take care of your sister…well, then I'll do all the special things. So, I guess I'm asking for two dates. Will you say yes?"

But she hesitated long enough to ask, "Why me?"

"Because of your love for your sister. And because you're so sexy. So, yes? No?"

"Yes," she said finally, telling herself he'd probably forget all about her as soon as they got out of here.

"Good. This first date, your sister is invited along. Let's have some hot drinks and see if we can't get some down her as well. And then I'm going to tell you what you made me realize about myself."

That instantly piqued her curiosity. He wouldn't let her help, but insisted on making coffee for them and tea for Cait. He also astonished her with a blueberry muffin.

"My weakness," he said as he put it in front of her on a napkin. "I never travel without them. I was saving them for dinner, but I think I have enough for us to have one now."

In spite of everything, she began to smile. When he brought the drinks, she woke Cait gently.

Chase pushed out of his seat and squatted beside Cait. "Hi, Cait. I'm Chase. I'm the guy who crashed the plane."

Cait blinked. Then she looked more closely at him, showing a spark of real interest that thrilled Rory. "I thought you saved us from crashing."

"Well, I couldn't exactly prevent it. But I wanted to ask your permission to date your sister."

At that a weak little laugh escaped Cait. Rory's heart swelled until she thought it would burst.

"Is that a yes?" Chase asked.

"Yes," Cait whispered. "If she agrees."

"I think she just did. Can you drink some tea? I made it special for you."

"Sure." Another whisper.

Chase reached for the cup on the table before Rory could, and brought it to Cait's lips. "You are one special lady," he said as Cait sipped.

"Me?" Cait looked surprised. "You don't know me."

"Ah, but we can judge people by those who care about them. Rory cares about you. A whole lot."

"I'm lucky."

"You're more than lucky. Lots of sisters don't like each other. So Rory's concern about you tells me all I need to know."

That elicited another smile from Cait. "I think I can hold the cup."

Rory helped her free her hands from the blankets and watched with easing tension as her sister drank. She was making an effort, and every effort she made was a commitment to live.

"Want to share my blueberry muffin?" Rory asked her. To Rory's great delight, Cait nodded.

Rory broke it into pieces and pushed the napkin over in front of Cait. Her sister put down her tea and picked up a small piece. "I'm so tired, but I'm getting hungry, too."

"That's good." Although it wasn't really. Cait had been on IV supplements that nobody had thought it was crucial to continue over the few hours it was supposed to have taken them to reach Minnesota. Of course she was getting hungry.

But Cait managed to consume nearly half the muffin and the whole cup of tea before coughing racked her again. Rory pounded her back the way Wendy had, and at last the coughing subsided, leaving Cait drained. Moments later she fell back to sleep.

Rory sat back, picked up her coffee mug and said with bitter frankness, "I hate myself."

"Why?"

"Because I wouldn't wait until I could hire an air ambulance. They'd have had IVs and all that stuff."

"Why didn't you wait?"

"No time." She shook her head, feeling a surge of frustration. "I had to get her there immediately or they wouldn't add her to the trial, because her doctors were saying she only had weeks left. I told you it was a hurdle to get her on this program. Well, the first air ambulance I could get wasn't for ten days. Nobody would bump another patient, one who was more likely to be saved by transport."

He nodded. "It's a hard calculus. I guess I'm used to it from the military."

"Triage. I get it. No one in Seattle held out any hope. So bumping some burn victim or desperately injured child wasn't going to happen. And I couldn't wait ten days because the researchers were flat-out frank about it. The longer the delay, the less they wanted her as a trial patient."

"More ugly calculus."

"Exactly. My sister's life was being weighed against the likelihood that anything might help her. I get it. I got it totally. So I asked what if I flew her on a private jet. None of the docs thought that was going to make anything worse. I've been wondering if that decision was solely because they considered her hopeless. Regardless, it was only supposed to be a few hours."

"Then don't hate yourself for not getting an ambulance. Dammit, Rory, what choice did you have?"

"I didn't think I had any."

"Well, you didn't. And if we hadn't crashed, she'd already be in the trial. How can you argue your decision now? You did the best you could under the circumstances."

"I know, I know. It's just that I'm looking at her now and thinking of all the things I wish I'd insisted on before we left. Like keeping her on IVs."

"I couldn't have transported her that way. So that would have taken you back to the ambulance solution. Which clearly would have prevented her from getting in the trial."

"I know." She bit her lip. "I know all of this logically."

"Then stop beating yourself up. Everything would have been just hunky-dory except for some lazy mechanic in Seattle who didn't do something right. Those are the kinds of things nobody can prepare for."

Rory drew a few deep breaths, fighting down her frustration. Being frustrated wouldn't change a thing. At last she let go of a long breath and tried to smile at Chase. "I thought this was supposed to be a date."

"It is. Who says you can't talk about things that upset you on a date? What kind of date would that be?"

"I don't know."

"Well, I do. It would be exactly the wrong kind. Exactly the kind of date I've gone on too often in my life. I said I was going to tell you something I'd realized about myself."

That completely captured her interest. "What's that?"

"That I got kicked to the curb a million times because I made a career out of picking the wrong kind of women. Over and over. And I think I did it on purpose."

"Meaning?"

"I had fighter-jock syndrome, for one thing. I looked at the outside of the package and made my selection from the unending deli of beauties who prowl the bars looking for guys like me. And then I picked the ones I knew wouldn't stick around."

"Why? Why would you do that?"

"I guess because I didn't want to get attached. I dunno. I'll have to think about that some. But watching you with Cait, I realized that you're the kind of person who will stick through thick and thin. That's what I wanted in my wingman. Why the hell wouldn't I want that in a woman?"

"Don't ask me. I have no idea. I know why I avoid involvement."

"Why's that?"

"Because it would lessen my authority if people are thinking about my sexuality. I'm already fighting an uphill battle."

"At least you understand why. I'm still working on it."

"Maybe you were just young and liked being foot-loose."

"And maybe I liked visiting the deli to try out a new sandwich." He gave a snort. "Don't think I'm proud of that."

"That doesn't make you unusual for a man."

"You might be right. Everyone I knew, with a few exceptions, was basically doing the same thing. Oh, they

tried marriage, the operative word often being *tried.*
Some found good relationships. A lot more wound up
divorced. We're not very good marriage risks, navy
pilots. Maybe it's different for the air force."

"That I wouldn't know."

"I don't have statistics to refer to," he admitted.
"But watching you with Cait, I suddenly realized that
I'd been getting exactly what I wanted from my girlfriends—desertion. And I don't think I want that anymore."

Her hand froze on her cup. Was he trying to tell her
something? God, she hoped not. She had enough on her
plate right now, and she didn't want to be another one
of the women who kicked him to curb.

"Anyway," he said after a moment, "a little self-
revelation. That's always good."

"I'm sure the women you're no longer blaming will
be relieved."

He chuckled quietly. "I think they were playing by
the same rules. I doubt a single one of them remembered me after I flew away."

"You make it sound like you were all counting coup."

"Maybe we were. Notches on the belt or something.
More coffee?"

He refilled their mugs and poured some more water
in the chafing dish that was still steaming on the table.
"Do we need to tent her again?"

Rory glanced at her watch. "Another ten minutes or
so."

"Okay."

He sat regarding Rory steadily. His stare made her
a bit uncomfortable, especially since she was remembering how he had touched her the night before, and
wishing he would do it again. The conflict between her

worry for her sister and this unexpected sexual need jarred her, but there it was.

Two sides of her nature, both trying to take charge. Well, one side *had* to be in charge. No way around it.

Then it struck her that he hadn't asked her to say anything about last night. No, he'd simply told her something that she would need to know later: that he hadn't just taken advantage of her because of proximity.

Later, whatever happened, that would reassure her that she hadn't just been used. The kindness of that was almost enough to take her breath away.

But he'd asked for no reassurance for himself. Didn't he need it? Or maybe he didn't want to hear her answer, was afraid she might say she'd just been having an adrenaline reaction.

Maybe she had been. But she doubted it. Truth was, sitting here across from him now, she still felt his magnetism. She still wanted to have sex with him. Out of place or not, there was no denying that it was real and she wanted more. With him. Only with him.

She hadn't felt that in a long, long time.

But she was afraid to tell him so. Afraid of what that might mean. There could be no future for them. She had to take care of Cait, then she had to get back to her job. Where could anyone else fit into that? Nothing had really changed—her job would make the same demands, and there'd be no place once again for thoughts of marriage and family. She *had* to believe this was just a passing desire or how would she ever get back to her career?

"Have some muffin," he said, nudging the napkin toward her. "This is a date, remember?"

"Certainly a memorable one."

He smiled. "We aim to please."

He helped with tenting Cait as he had promised, and they got her to cough some more. They even got her to drink another cup of heavily sweetened tea.

"I thought you two were having a date," Cait said breathlessly as she sagged back in the seat.

"Shh," Rory said, holding the tea to her lips.

"No." Cait gave another small cough. "This is something I never thought I'd live to see. My sister on a date."

"In a crashed plane," Chase pointed out. "With the pilot who was at the helm. At least we have the candle-light to add to the romance, though."

Cait actually laughed. It dissolved into coughs, but when she caught her breath again she looked at Rory. "I think," she said faintly, "that I want to live."

Rory's heart cracked as surely as if it had been cleaved in two. Her throat grew so tight she couldn't answer.

"That's good news," Chase said gently. "We'll get you to Minnesota, Cait. We will."

Her sister looked at a man she didn't even know, and Rory saw the trust in her gaze. "I believe you."

"Then how about some more tea or muffin? Gotta keep your strength up."

But the clock just kept ticking, and to Rory it sounded like the heartbeat of horror: loud and echo-ing. Time kept running out like grains of sand in an hourglass, and more endless hours stretched ahead of them before they could do a damn thing.

Time, the cruelest taskmaster of all.

Chapter 8

The day outside brightened steadily, but the snow showed no evidence of abating. The plane rocked a little as afternoon arrived, and Rory guessed that the buried wing had been blown clear again.

Her nerves grew tighter, ready to shriek from the inactivity. God, she couldn't stand this. Cait might be worsening, to judge by her congestion, and Rory just wasn't built to sit around twiddling her thumbs, which was about all she could do right now.

Playing cards didn't distract her nearly enough, and even the funny stories Chase tried to tell about the military filled only small pieces of endless time.

Except time wasn't endless. It might feel like it right now, but it was short—shorter than she could stand to think about.

Every time she looked at her sister, she questioned her judgments and decisions. Not only about deciding to take a private flight to save time, but about how to handle this situation when the storm passed.

Should they wait if the GPS came up, assuming the beacon was undamaged? How much more might they risk by stumbling out into the snowy mountainside? Would the exposure put Cait at even greater risk?

There were no answers. None at all.

She had believed that she had learned to live by the maxim *Worry about the things you can fix, and not the things you can't.* Yeah, she could do that when it came to her job. She had a lot of control there, and when control was taken from her it was often by someone who employed her, and the problem then became theirs.

But this was different, so different from anything she had faced before. Her coping skills fell far short of having learned to wait.

"You need to nap," Chase told her.

Wendy and Yuma were in the galley, making more hot soup to be followed by tenting Cait again.

"I don't want to be alone." The bald admission startled Rory. She was *used* to being alone. She basically lived her life alone, relying only on herself. She thought of herself as strong, independent, a woman who could travel the world and work under nearly all conditions.

And now she was falling apart, feeling weak, frightened and afraid of failing. So unlike her. She wished she could snatch back the revealing words, but even if Chase hadn't been there to hear them, she *had*. Now she stared starkly at herself, at the facade she had created over the years, and realized there were other parts of her long unnourished. Parts she didn't want. Parts she wished she could sever.

"Okay," Chase said. "After we eat, I'll nap with you. You know Wendy can look after Cait."

In fact, Wendy had been far more useful in looking after Cait than Rory had been. She wouldn't have known how to handle her sister's growing congestion. Wouldn't have been able to listen to her sister's chest and judge the gravity of it.

"I guess we're lucky there was a nurse onboard," she said.

"Very." Chase gave her a half smile. "A damn fine nurse. She's dealt with a lot worse in emergencies."

Rory didn't want to imagine worse. This was certainly bad enough.

They chatted about nothing substantial during their meal, avoiding any discussion about the situation. Cait ate another full cup of soup, and then cleared her lungs again. Only when she at last slipped back into sleep did Rory feel that she could go nap herself.

But she wasn't at all sure she'd sleep. Wound as tight as a coiled spring, every muscle in her body was tense enough to ache. She slipped under the covers in the chilly aft cabin, and stared at the fuselage only inches away, almost invisible as only a little light reached the room from the candles in the main cabin.

She knew she needed to sleep. At any moment something could change, and the better rested she was, the better she would be able to handle it. Fitfully dozing last night had not left her feeling rested. But would anything?

A few minutes later, Chase entered the cabin. She heard him close the door, move around a bit, and then he slipped in behind her, wrapping his arms around her.

God, it felt good to be held. So good. How could she have forgotten the soothing power of a simple hug? It had been so long since she had allowed anyone to do this.

"Relax," he murmured. "We'll be the first to know if something happens."

That was true, and acceptance of that allowed her to uncoil just a bit. He helped by running his hand soothingly along the length of her side, from shoulder to knee. As if he were petting her.

With her head pillowed on his arm, his other hand stroking her gently, she closed her eyes and willed herself to relax.

The anxiety that had been winding her steadily tighter since she had learned of Cait's illness, and ever more rapidly since the crash, began to ease.

Surely it wouldn't be a crime to let go of worry for just a little while. Especially since she was helpless to do anything about it.

And as she relaxed, weariness began to rise. God, she was worn out. Worn out from the last few weeks, worn out from all her terrors and all her efforts, worn out from the last twenty-four hours and all the added complications.

"Chase?"

"Hmm?"

"She's all I have left."

"I gathered that."

"I don't know what I'll do." A tear rolled down her cheek, just one, hot against her cold skin. "Maybe it's stupid, but even after we lost Mom and Dad, Cait was always there in my mind. Like an anchor. I still had family."

He made a sound like agreement.

"I wish you'd met Cait when she was well."

"Was she like you?"

"That depends on what you mean."

"Feisty, determined, dedicated," he said.

"That's an overestimation of me."

"We can argue about it another time. Tell me about Cait."

"She's softhearted. I don't mean that in a bad way, either. Just that she was the one who'd bring home the stray cat or dog, who'd get upset even about killing a spider."

"Really?"

A choked laugh escaped Rory. "You will never know how many times I had to agree to try to capture bugs before I was allowed to step on them. We had a problem with pygmy rattlesnakes in our yard for a while, and what with the dogs she'd brought home, Mom and Dad were worried one of the dogs might get a snakebite. But Cait would go out with a shovel and scoop them up and toss them back into the woods."

"So she *is* like you."

"I dunno. At that age I was all for killing them."

"But you didn't."

"No." She sighed. "I guess at some level I was glad she protected them. Yes, they were a threat, but if they could be safely removed, why kill them? As she was fond of saying, 'They're just being snakes doing snaky things.'"

"And when she got older?"

"Pretty much the same. Rescuing animals. Until she became sick, she worked for a rescue organization. She got married, talked about having four kids, and in the process of trying to find out why she couldn't get pregnant they discovered the lymphoma."

She sighed, and used a corner of the blanket to wipe away that stray tear. "She was all about helping. Helping people, helping animals. I couldn't even list all the charities she volunteered for. She's one of the last people this world can afford to lose. Me, I just went off to do my own thing because finding oil challenged me. I looked for the excitement, I guess. She looked for love."

"She sounds pretty special."

"She is."

"Here." He tugged her gently until she rolled over so that they were face-to-face. There was no light in the bedroom, except what seeped around the door from the candles in the main cabin. Even so, she could just make out his features.

"You've done everything humanly possible," he told her. "I admire that."

"What if I've failed?"

"It won't be for lack of trying. You can be proud of that. No one on this planet can promise you the outcome you want, so whatever happens, it's hardly failure."

"Maybe not." But her heart ached and she squeezed her eyes closed.

He tightened his arms around her. "Right now you have to let go. I swear, as soon as this storm passes, we'll figure out what's the best thing to do, and we'll do it. You're not alone in this, Rory. I promise. I'll help every way I can, every step of the way."

God, how long had it been since someone had said she wasn't alone with something? Maybe it was her own fault—her need to control—but she never relied on other people to do more than the bare minimum. That was a far cry from someone telling you that he'd be with you, that you weren't alone.

All of a sudden she felt frightened again, but for a very different reason. She realized that she had armored herself against needing anyone or anything, seeing it as a weakness. Mostly she had feared that others, who already wanted to put her down because she was a woman, would see it as weakness and try to take advantage of her.

Right now she felt that protective shell trying to crack open, and she was terrified that if it did she might never be able to put it back together.

"Rory? You're shaking."

But not from cold. Sheer terror gripped her, terror that she had been holding at bay for weeks now. She was out of her element, she was helpless and she was dependent on others. Something had at last risen up in her life to show her that, in the end, nobody could do it all alone.

No matter how tough she was, no matter how much in charge she was, no matter how she tried to wrest what she wanted or needed from the world around her, she couldn't always rely on her own determination, stubbornness, intelligence and strength. Sometimes she needed help.

She had always been a fighter. She had always gotten what she wanted, including getting Cait into this clinical trial, even though she didn't strictly fit the criteria. She fought, and she usually won, because she wouldn't quit, and because she could always find a way.

Not this time. Not in a crashed plane on a mountainside. There was nothing she could do to change this situation.

These past few weeks she had been trying to avoid facing this. She had tried to force a system to give Cait back her health, even though they all kept telling her they couldn't do anything. She had battled to get Cait into this clinical trial against all odds, and had succeeded. Then their plane crashed. Then they were lost on the side of a mountain with no assurance that they could get Cait out of here no matter what anyone did.

But of one thing she was certain: none of the traits she prided herself on would allow her to solve this alone.

Just as once she entered Cait in the trial it would be out of her hands.

She had refused to think about that. Refused to acknowledge that sooner or later she would become helpless to do more. She didn't allow herself such thoughts, ever.

But she couldn't escape them any longer.

"Rory?" His voice, pitched low, was gentle.

"I'm so scared," she admitted brokenly. "I can't fix anything. I can't do anything. I'm helpless."

He took a few moments before responding. "We're all pretty helpless right now. That's going to change during the night. Then we're all going to pull together, and you'll be able to do plenty. I'm counting on it."

She sighed, trying to release tension, and failing. "That's not exactly it."

"Then tell me."

"I'm used to being in control. One way or another, I deal with problems, and I solve them. And right now I can't do that, and when you said you'd help me, I realized how little help I've accepted or even wanted over the years, and it just…just…" She couldn't go on.

"I see." Again he pondered for a minute or two. "One of the things you learn in the military is that you're part of a team. Even a fighter jock doesn't get off the runway without a lot of support from the ground crew and the tower. Everyone plays a key role. Then when you get in the air, your life can depend on your wingman if there's trouble. I guess I'm used to relying on others."

She sighed again, trying to absorb what he was saying.

"You don't have to be alone. And right now we're all pretty helpless. We have to lean on each other. There's no other way to get through this, Rory. And that's not a sign of weakness."

She almost gasped. "How did you know I was thinking about that?"

"Maybe I read minds. I don't know. Maybe because I've known control freaks before. They only feel safe when they do everything themselves, and depend only on themselves."

"I am a control freak," she admitted. "I thought of it as being strong, but it's not that. I don't dare depend on others."

"And now you have to. We're all leaning on each right now. There's no weakness in that. In fact, it's how we become stronger, by working together."

"I've been part of teams," she argued.

"But I'll bet you were the boss."

"Usually," she admitted.

"This time there's no boss, except maybe Yuma. He knows these mountains and how to survive in these conditions better than anyone. But we'll still be pulling together once this storm passes and we figure out what we need to do."

She bit her lip, gnawing on it just as she was gnawing on the upheaval inside her. She'd always been afraid of leaning on others, because what if they failed? Yet here she was, unable to do anything else. Maybe, a little voice in her head said, she just needed to get over herself. Things were complicated enough without twisting herself into knots over needing help. And wasn't she proposing to lean on doctors in Minnesota? Sheesh, she wasn't making sense at all.

"I suppose," she said tremulously, "that I could call this a life lesson."

"Maybe. They always seem to hurt."

"Yeah."

He drew her a little closer, hugging her tighter. "One of the things I had to face was that I wasn't indestructible. I mean, you've gotta have a tremendous sense of invincibility to be a fighter jock. Then one day they tell you there's some little squiggle on your EKG, it's meaningless but hey, buddy, you can't fly those planes anymore."

"Ouch." She could easily imagine that, actually.

"Yeah, ouch is right. All of a sudden you're not invincible. The years are creeping up on you and you've just lost the thing you thought you were living for. It doesn't help when they tell you it happens to nearly everyone by your age, and that they're just being hypercautious. Doesn't help one bit."

"No, it wouldn't. I'm sorry, Chase."

"Thanks. But I've made the adjustment and I'm mostly content. Now *you're* making an adjustment. There are some things—important things—that you can't control. So we're going to be operating as a team."

His logic reached her brain, but her heart was struggling to accept it. She hated the weakness and helplessness she felt now, and yet he was telling her she was no more weak or helpless than any of them. Maybe he was right. Maybe it was time to grow up and face the fact that not everything in life would bend to her will or her expertise.

"I've been deluding myself," she said after a bit.

"How?"

"Thinking I needed no one. That I was a solitary pillar capable of shouldering any burden. Apparently I'm not."

"That's not a bad thing, because none of us are that strong."

"No." She drew a long breath. "I started thinking about this when I realized just how much it meant to me when you offered to stand by me. I can't remember the last time someone offered me that, and that's when I realized it's because I don't allow it."

"Maybe it's time to offer a little trust, and let someone help."

"I have no choice now."

She wished the words unspoken as soon as they left her mouth. She felt him stiffen and draw back a little. Amazing how much that small withdrawal pained her.

"That came out wrong," she said quickly. "I didn't mean it the way it sounded."

"Then how did you mean it?"

"That I think I have no choice but to learn a lesson I probably should have learned a long time ago."

She felt him relax and was more relieved than she cared to admit. She didn't want this man to pull away from her, not even a trifle. Nor did she want to think about why she felt that way. Just let it be. For now. If she could do that as necessary on her job, why not in personal matters? She put that question away for another time, too. She sensed, however, that somewhere in there was a key to her nature that needed some attention.

Odd that she felt so close to him, though. Not just physically, but emotionally. She never would have expected that when she boarded this plane, or even directly after the crash. Something about him, however, seemed engagingly open and inviting. She got the sense that he was long past playing games with himself or anyone else.

How did you get there, she wondered, because it had never been clearer to her that she had been playing her own game, pretending to need no one and nothing.

Hell, maybe she'd even been using memories of her sister, awareness that she still *had* a sister, all these years to keep herself from feeling totally adrift, even though she hadn't visited often enough.

No, she wasn't going to beat herself up about that now. Enough, already. She couldn't change the past— she could only resolve to do better from now on. She had a feeling, though, that earthquakes were going to be rattling through her psyche for a long time after this.

Sleep eluded her, though, as her mind tried to race in useless circles, worrying over the things she'd learned about herself, worrying about things beyond her control. Damn, she wished her brain had an off switch.

Apparently it did. As if he sensed her continued tension, Chase began rubbing her back gently. Instinctively, she moved closer, every other thought forgotten as she became instantly aroused.

How could he do that to her?

But she didn't care. At first she welcomed it as a relief from the places she'd been wandering, but it wasn't long before it went past welcome to hunger and need.

Nor was it just a means of escape, she realized just before his mouth settled over hers. In her deepest being, she was certain that she would have wanted him under any circumstances. Any circumstances at all.

And these weren't the best. A slim door to give them

privacy, a room that was too chilly, danger lurking…
and dammit, she wanted him.

She raised her arm to hug him back, and heard a
quiet murmur of approval from him. She didn't know
what they were doing, if they were making a mistake,
and she absolutely didn't care.

She wanted Chase, he wanted her, and that seemed
like the answer to nearly every question in the universe
right then.

He hadn't kissed her before, but he kissed her now as
if her mouth were all he wanted. He teased her tongue
with his, traced her lips with it, then dove in for a
deeper kiss. She was oh so ready for it, the rhythmic
movement of tongue against tongue, tasting faintly of
coffee. It seemed so right that in these endless, dangerous, helpless hours that they should seek to express
something beautiful, something life-affirming.

When she could welcome him no more deeply with
her mouth, he rolled them a bit, so that he rose over her
on one elbow.

"Stop me now," he murmured against her lip. "Now
or never."

"Don't stop," she whispered. "Oh, please, don't stop."

Given permission, he didn't hesitate. His hand
slipped up under her sweater, cold against her midriff.
She shivered with delight as much as with the cold
touch, but he was patient. He let his hand warm against
her while he trailed kissed across her cheeks, her throat,
her ear and then captured her mouth again.

Their tongues dueled as if they had been born for
this moment. Never had a kiss felt so right. Then his
hand stole upward.

He found the front clasp of her bra and set her free.

* * *

Cupping her breast, Chase felt the lightning bolt of heat shoot through him to his groin. She felt surprisingly full in his hand, and her nipple was as hard as a pebble. Feeling it against his palm nearly dragged a groan from him.

He squeezed gently, until she writhed against him, then he brushed her nipple with his thumb. A shiver passed through her and into him. Between his legs he felt hot and heavy, ready. More than ready.

But he didn't want to rush this. He had to battle an urge to just take her now, claim her now, make her his now, because he felt an equally strong urge to carry her every step of the way with him.

There was only one road to heaven at the moment, and this was it. He was going to make sure she came with him.

Besides, he was feeling unusually protective of her. He hadn't felt this way about a lover before. His partners in bed had always been experienced, always knowing what they were doing, and never wounded or hurt.

But he felt a deep hurt in Rory, one that went beyond her sister's illness. That hurt made her vulnerable, and he was determined that she not walk away from this time feeling used. No, he wanted her to feel worshipped. Adored. Cherished.

With the blood throbbing in his head and his body, he couldn't analyze those feelings now. They just were. When a soft moan escaped her and her body arched against his, he knew there would be no stopping. She was ready right now, but he wasn't going to allow this to be rough and graceless like last night. There might not be any roses or champagne, but they weren't what mattered anyway. What mattered was how he treated her now.

He took his time. He tormented her by holding back. And he almost chuckled when she pressed her breast harder into his hand, signaling her need unmistakably.

It was chilly in the cabin, but he suspected neither of them much cared right now. He pushed her sweater up, baring her breasts, wishing only that he could see their delights as well as feel them. A shudder ripped through her, and then again as he found her nipple with his mouth.

"Ahh..." It was little more than a sigh, but it told him enough. He sucked gently at first, teasing her nipple with his tongue, liking the contrast of its hardness compared to the softness of her breast. Liking the way it felt both soft and rough against his tongue.

She writhed, pressing harder against him from head to toe, and the ache within him grew to massive proportions.

It had been a long time since he'd come this close to losing control, but something about this woman put him on the very brink.

He paused just a moment, fighting down his own needs, determined to give her everything she could possibly want in these circumstances. Then he found her breast again, sucking even harder, as if he wanted to draw her inside him. A little nip for good measure and she arched so hard against him that he almost lost it.

God, she was sexy, and good and... Rational thought abandoned him.

Rory had never guessed how exquisitely sensitive her breasts could be, but Chase was rapidly teaching her that every other experience in her life had been pale by comparison.

It had been way too long since a man had touched her this way. Too long since she had even considered allowing it. It was as if pent-up years of self-denial were exploding all at once.

Her nipples were acutely sensitive, the one in his mouth responding to his ministrations, the other puckering in eagerness in the chilly air, the merest brush against it sending spikes of sheer desire to her very core.

She throbbed, she ached, she grew damp, and they'd barely started. She never wanted it to end.

Finally, he tore his mouth from her and trailed it up her chest, her throat, to give her another kiss. "It's cold in here," he whispered finally. "I don't want to go fast, but I don't want you to get chilled."

She didn't think that was possible. She was also in no mood to wait. Right now that was a luxury that didn't appeal to her at all.

"Hurry," she whispered back. "Oh, please, just hurry."

She hardly cared how cold the air felt when he rose, taking the blanket with him. She could hear him struggling to strip in the dark. Then his hands tugged at her clothing and she fought to help him. She wanted it all gone, every bit of it.

Wanted to know the delicious feeling of his skin pressed to hers from head to foot. Wanted to know everything about how he felt, and how he could make her feel.

As soon as he'd pulled her jeans and panties from her, he spread the blankets over her again. Then, surprising her, he burrowed in near her feet.

"Oh…" It was barely a breath as she felt him kiss the insteps of her feet, then her arches. Inch by inch he made his way up her legs, kissing and licking here and there. Making even that ordinary skin feel like an instrument of exquisite pleasure.

Anticipation built in her, a violent but steady drumbeat. Steadily, he moved upward, approaching that most secret of places, the part of her that felt as if it were expanding, opening, crying out silently for fullness.

Then he found her, dropping kisses on her swollen, moist petals. She bit back a groan, trying to hold still so that it would never stop, but her body betrayed her, tipping her hips up toward him.

At once he pressed his face hard against her, then a sharp shaft of pleasure-pain speared through her as his tongue found that exquisitely sensitive knot of nerves. It was almost too much to bear, and only some dim remaining sense kept her from screaming out at the sensation.

Never before…

None of this had ever happened before. He licked her again and it almost seemed as if something grabbed her, forcing her hips upward for more and more. She was afraid it would end. She feared she couldn't handle much more. So intense. So extreme. So utterly unimaginable…

Again, then again, and just as she thought she would shatter into a million billion flaming pieces in painful pleasure, he stopped. He left her hanging on the precipice.

But not for long. Not for long at all.

He slid up and over her, his staff seeking entrance. She reached down to help him, finding him sheathed in latex, knowing a momentary pang that there was something between them, however necessary.

And then he slipped into her, filling her, answering that ache for his swollen member. How could she have forgotten how good it felt to be filled and stretched this way? Had it *ever* felt this good?

His mouth clamped to her breast again, making her feel as she were one long wire of exquisite feeling, as if nothing existed but his hardness driving into her and his mouth tormenting her.

He plunged again and again, rotating gently in a way that caressed her swollen knot of nerves.

Higher and higher until…until everything vanished except the peak they strove for. Until nothing existed but the pleasure between them.

She sucked in a sharp breath, feeling it happen. Nerve endings exploded everywhere, a hard ache turning to incredible release that rolled through her like ocean wave after ocean wave.

Endlessly.

"Damn, Rory," he panted by her ear. "Damn."

She doubted that she could move a muscle. Talking seemed like way too much effort. "Something wrong?" she managed thickly.

"God, no! I've never…"

"Me, either," she mumbled.

He groaned. "Sorry."

She almost protested when he rolled off her. She didn't want him gone, but understood. She was growing cold. He had to take care of things.…

It was the cold that brought her completely back. He found a candle on one of the shelves and lit it. By its dim flickering light, he untangled the heap of clothes on the floor and quickly started helping her to dress.

As soon as she was clothed again, he donned his own garments. Then he laid down with her and pulled the blankets over them, snuggling her close as warmth returned.

"You're amazing," he murmured, and kissed her.

"So are you. I've never…" She didn't want to say it, but she didn't need to.

She snuggled into his embrace, her head in the hollow of his shoulder. "Thank you for everything."

"I think you got that the wrong way around."

"I hope you think so."

He squeezed her and shifted a bit so that his leg lay between hers. "I really do want to date you after all this is cleared up."

"I'd like that."

"I mean, I realize it'll be tough with you a country away and all, but I *do* have wings."

"You'll need to persuade some of your clients to check out the oil biz in Mexico. All so that we can eat tortillas and drink tequila together."

"Oh, I think we'll do more than eat tortillas."

She smiled. "Probably."

"No probably about it. Now try to get some sleep, darlin'. We'll have plenty of time to talk later."

Now she didn't want to sleep for another reason. She wanted to savor the afterglow, to remember each detail of what had just happened so she could take it out and enjoy it again and again no matter what happened.

But she really hadn't had enough sleep, and despite her efforts to hold it off, it claimed her almost without warning.

* * *

Wendy and Yuma let them sleep until suppertime. When Rory emerged from the bedroom, having stepped in the bathroom to wash quickly with some paper towels and icy water, she found Cait awake and sipping another hot beverage. Playing cards were laid out, even in front of Cait.

"She's been playing rummy with us," Wendy said brightly.

Something in that bright tone alerted Rory. She took a second look at Wendy. "What?"

"Cait's a little more congested. We've been working on it."

That didn't sound good, but Rory didn't want to ask in front of Cait for fear of adding to her stress. "Should I tent her more often?"

"Yeah," Wendy said. "And if she starts to sound tight again, wake me, okay?"

That was not good. The last lingering bit of afterglow fled as she slid into a seat beside Cait. "Playing rummy, huh?"

Cait gave a little nod. "Sort of. They were helping me."

Rory studied her sister's face and didn't like what she saw. Cait's eyes appeared too bright, and her color, so pale for so long, had risen. Fever. She wanted to reach out and check, but again hesitated for fear of adding to Cait's concerns. She glanced up at Chase and saw him frowning.

"I'm going to go try the damn radio and GPS again," he said. "I'll be back shortly."

So he was worried enough to struggle with equipment, even though he knew it probably wouldn't work until the storm had passed. Or even then.

Because it was beginning to seem to Rory, although she was no expert, that the amount of atmospheric disturbance required to keep them totally out of touch this long was probably not normal.

And Chase's march into the cockpit seemed to substantiate that.

When he returned twenty minutes later, he gave her a shake of his head. "We need to eat."

A totally different topic. And now her fears had ratcheted up another notch, something she would have thought impossible. Guilt speared her, too. When she had gone to take her nap, Cait had actually seemed a little better, a little stronger. Now she could only kick herself for not being beside her sister when she was obviously getting sicker.

It was a stupid thought, as if she could have prevented this. Wendy had done everything possible while they were stuck in this trap. She didn't doubt it, so why beat herself up over it?

Yuma had apparently made dinner before waking them. Chase heated what was left over with candles. Cait stirred and agreed to another cup of tea.

It was so little to do for her sister, so very little. She felt the worst urge to indulge in a primal scream just to ease the tension.

Chase brought out more muffins, too. Rory ate without tasting, in between getting more sips of heavily sweetened tea into Cait, and encouraging her to eat some muffin.

"I never ate so much sweet stuff at one time," Cait whispered.

"Enjoy. They'll probably take it all away from you again at the hospital."

Cait managed a smile, then started coughing again. Rory definitely didn't like the sound of it.

"I'll get the tent," Chase said immediately.

Once again Rory huddled under the survival blanket while steam filled it from the chafing dish, holding her sister's hand and pounding her back every few minutes.

Cait's congestion had increased; Rory could hear it. Worse, her cough sounded tighter. *Pneumonia.* The dreaded word could no longer be pushed away.

Finally, exhaustion claimed Cait, taking her into slumber so deep it approached unconsciousness. Rory sat awhile longer, waving steam toward her sister's face, but no more coughs came.

At last she pushed away the blanket and looked at Chase. "We've got to get out of here."

"I know. But not in the dark. Not until the storm stops. It won't do anyone a damn bit of good—least of all Cait—if we go out there, get lost, break legs…"

"I know, I know. I just want some mercy. Just a little mercy." It sounded exactly like the plea it was: a cry straight from her soul.

He nodded, his mouth tightening.

But what could he say? Not a word. "Eat up," he said after a moment. "You need to pack in as many calories as you can. We may well be hiking out of here early."

She nodded. She didn't want to think of all the difficulties that would face them in these mountains. But if the plane wasn't sending out a locator signal, they couldn't afford to wait. Not now.

Her heart sank to her toes.

Chapter 9

It happened during the wee hours. Rory had refused to leave Cait's side even to sleep, so she was dozing beside her sister. A groan awoke her and for a few seconds she couldn't identify it.

She turned at once to Cait, who still slept, and noticed that her breathing sounded a little raspy, but not terrible. Evidently, she hadn't made that sound.

Then it came again. Chase, who had been slumbering across the aisle sat bolt upright. "Hell," he said.

"Chase?"

He didn't answer. He jumped up immediately and went to get Wendy and Yuma. A few minutes later they stumbled out of the back cabin, carrying their boots.

"Everybody get dressed. Everything you've got, as many layers as you can. Rory, if you have an extra set of thermal stuff, get it on Cait."

She did. Why she had an extra set, she didn't know.

At the time she'd bought it, she'd wondered, but for some reason had felt compelled. Maybe because she'd been worried about how cold she would get in Minnesota when she was used to Mexico.

Wendy helped her before finishing her own dressing. They dug out more survival blankets and tucked them along with every available blanket around Cait.

"What's happening?" Rory demanded even as she worked.

"I'm not sure, but I think we're about to move."

"Why?"

"Yeah," Yuma said. "Doesn't it usually get colder behind a storm?"

"I don't know," Chase said flatly. "I don't know. But I feel something…" He told them all to buckle into their seats.

Then he blew out the candles and they waited.

For a long time nothing happened. Then she heard another groan from the metal around them. Her heart slammed, because this time she thought she felt movement. It was hard to be sure, but her body seemed to have felt a slight slip, the smallest increase in pressure of her back against the seat.

She gripped the arms of her chair until her fingers ached, her heart rapidly pounding, and waited… waited…

The next few minutes felt like eternity. Just as she began to hope that nothing more would happen, it did.

There was a sudden slip, a shriek from metal, she knew a few moments of dizziness, a lurching feeling, and the next thing she was aware of was snow blowing in her face.

She opened her eyes, but could see nothing at all.

"Nobody move," Chase barked. "It might not be over."

He was right. Another lurch, another scream from the plane, more icy air and snow whipping about her.

Then she felt as if she were riding on one of those circular sleds, round and round like a top, only not as fast. A huge crunching sound rent the night, then it all came to a sudden halt that threw her sideways and made her seat belt tight.

Then nothing. For a long, long time, nothing except the cold and blowing snow. She felt as if she couldn't catch her breath.

A light snapped on. Chase had a flashlight. He was still belted into a seat and she could just make him out as he played the beam around the cabin.

She followed the light, gasping in horror as she saw that the fuselage had torn open. And somehow, impossibly, the very back of the plane seemed to have filled with snow.

"Don't anybody else move," Chase said. "I can't be sure it's over. Rory, make sure Cait's face is covered."

She leaned over, aided by his flashlight, and drew one of the blankets over Cait's face. Amazingly, Cait seemed to have slept through it all. Not good. In fact, terrible. No one should have been able to sleep through that. That frightened Rory so much she leaned over to make sure her sister was still breathing. Yes, she was, but it didn't sound good.

Chase shined the light on his watch. "Dawn in two hours. I think our options just grew more limited."

"I agree," Yuma said. "We just lost our shelter."

The protection the plane had provided was gone. They were exposed now, as exposed as if they had walked out into the storm.

"It doesn't seem to be blowing anywhere near as hard now," Chase remarked. "It must almost be over."

But the rest had only just begun.

They waited a long time before Chase was convinced that they were probably done moving, at least for a while. Rory jumped up when he said he was going out to see what had happened. She looked at Wendy, who nodded toward Cait, signaling that she would watch her.

Never built to just wait, Rory joined Chase and Yuma as they clambered through the cracked hull to examine what had happened.

The plane had turned around somehow as it slid, and had broken in two places: just forward of the port wing and at the tail. In fact, it looked as if the tail had been sheared off as it swung around and hit the trees that earlier had looked so far away.

"One of the wings must've lifted on the wind," Chase said. "Right as the plane started to slip."

They walked back upslope and surveyed the path of the slip. Clearly, the snow under the plane had turned into a sheet of ice. Combined with a few gusts of wind, that had been enough.

"I guess we're lucky it didn't happen sooner," Yuma remarked.

"I guess."

But Rory noticed something else. "The snow is stopping. The air feels warmer, or am I imagining it?"

Chase paused and lifted his face. "You're right."

"If it's been warming," Yuma said, "that would explain the slip. We were probably frozen in place until then."

"Maybe," Chase agreed. "Okay, we need to get it

together. We're going to have to leave. This isn't shelter anymore, it's just additional danger. So we've got to gather everything we possibly can, and we need to make a stretcher. Or find a way to tie Cait to my back like a papoose."

Rory didn't object. As sick as Cait was getting, she didn't want to wait. Plus, it seemed to her they'd all be warmer if they kept moving than they would be if they tried to sit it out now.

They'd lost their shelter. That didn't leave a whole lot of options.

Now that the storm was abating, Chase tried the radio and the GPS once more. Nothing. Somehow, some way, those devices were dead. If any beacon was still broadcasting, it would require homing in on.

"I figure that if they get anywhere close to the plane, they'll find us. I've got flares to signal if we see a search plane."

"Agreed," said Yuma, and Rory nodded.

Especially, she thought, since the wind kept blowing, and even from inside the remains of the cabin she could see that the plane was rapidly being buried once again.

At first light, they were ready to go. Rory put her own jacket on Cait, who was wrapped in layers of blankets, to protect her from the dry air and cold. For herself, she just piled on every other piece of clothing she had, and accepted Wendy's extra knit hat, scarf and gloves.

"Once we get into the woods," Yuma said, "there'll be a lot less wind." He stood outside for a few minutes, looking around as daylight revealed the terrain. It had stopped snowing completely, though the sky was still clouded and the snow on the ground kept blowing around.

"The clouds are good, right?" Rory said.

"They'll keep the temperature from dropping suddenly," Chase agreed. "At this time of the year, it usually gets colder when they clear out."

"Small blessings."

"I'll take every one I can get."

So would she.

"I think I know where we are," Yuma said. "If I'm right, and we head downhill, we should hit a county road."

He didn't say how long that would take, nor did Rory ask. She decided that for once she was better off not knowing some things.

There was a road out there. She made up her mind that they were going to reach it come hell or high water.

Amazing everyone, Chase dug some bungee cords out of one of the now-twisted overhead bins. "What?" he said when he realized that everyone was staring at him.

"Is there nothing you don't have on that plane?" Rory asked.

"These are handier than you would believe. I use them all the time. And now we can use them to secure Cait to my back. Maybe later to a stretcher if that seems like a good idea."

Pretty soon every pocket was stuffed with something, from food packs to lighters, and even a first-aid kit. Wendy and Yuma had been traveling with duffels and backpacks instead of suitcases, and those proved extremely handy.

By the time they took their first steps away from

the plane, Rory felt they had gathered everything they possibly could carry that might be of use.

She looked back once as they walked away from the plane. It had been good to them, she thought as she watched it get buried even deeper in blowing snow. It had saved their lives.

Now they had to save their own.

They reached the forest after only ten minutes, despite the deep snow. Once under the thick boughs, the wind nearly vanished, and the blanket of snow thinned appreciably.

Rory had only one concern. "No one could see us in the trees."

"It's okay," Chase said. "I have the flare gun. We hear a plane, we shoot."

"Okay."

"Then," said Yuma, "we hunt up a clearing. There are lots of them. But right now we can't afford the exposure of open ground, or the risk of avalanche."

Rory's heart skipped a beat. "I hadn't even thought about avalanches."

"The safest place to be is in thick woods," Yuma answered. "Take it off your worry list."

"I guess I do have a whole list."

Wendy patted her arm. "So would I, in your shoes."

Yuma led the way, heartening her with his confidence. He seemed to know where they were, and which was the best way to go. He did pick up a tall stick, though, and she watched him use it to test the ground ahead of him, looking for dips that might have been hidden beneath the snow.

Every so often, they paused and Rory checked on

Cait. Her hands remained warm, her face didn't feel chilled, but her breathing rattled.

She and Wendy pounded Cait's back without untying her from Chase, and managed to clear out her lungs a bit, but not enough.

"Another hour," Wendy said. "Another hour and we've got to tent her."

"Consider it done," Yuma answered. He picked up the pace.

Rory's mind scrambled around frantically. They had to ease Cait's breathing, but every stop to build a fire was going to slow their progress. For the first time she realized how fortunate they had been to have the plane's protection. All the frenzy she had felt to be on the move and seeking help had partially blinded her to their good fortune.

Now the threat was not the lymphoma—it was pneumonia. Her sister could die on this trek, no matter what they did. How had she ever thought hiking out of here would be better than waiting?

But they had no choice now. None. The plane had become dangerous as a shelter, open to the elements. They had to strive to make it to a road. They could do nothing else.

On another day, under other circumstances, she might have noticed the beauty of the woods around them, the evergreens and snow. So appropriate for the season. But she couldn't care less about the season, and had no sense of the beauty. All she knew was that they had to keep moving as quickly as possible.

She was so unaccustomed to the altitude that it fatigued her as much as the uneven terrain and the snow she had to wade through. She hated to admit it, but when they stopped to build a small fire, heat some food and tent Cait, she needed the rest nearly as much as her sister.

The tenting was more difficult now, as the wind managed to occasionally find them. They had untied Cait from Chase's back, then set her on Rory's lap.

"You're not used to the altitude," Wendy said. "You need the humidity almost as much as she does."

She held her sister on her crossed legs, making a chair for her, keeping her off the icy ground. Another survival blanket had been tucked beneath her for protection, but while she didn't get wet from the snow, it scarcely felt warm at first.

Chase had managed to pack the chafing dish and snow melted quickly in it over a very small fire. They propped the tent on some tree limbs, keeping it above the ground just enough to admit oxygen, but soon it grew almost cozy inside, and filled with steam that immediately began to bead on the silvery blanket.

Cait moaned softly and began to really awaken. "What's going on?"

Earlier she had been only half-awake, and quietly accepting, but now she seemed to become aware of the change in scenery.

"We're hiking down the mountain to help. And you need to cough," Rory said firmly. "No matter how tired you are, you *have* to cough. Please, Cait. Please."

"'Kay."

But it seemed like a long time before she even attempted it. Just as Rory's concern began to reach a fever pitch, she heard the first tight cough. A moment later came a small one that sounded looser.

At once the tent was removed from Rory's head and tucked between her and Cait.

"Let's go," Wendy said. "Lean her forward so I can reach her, or lean back yourself."

Rory wasn't sure Cait would remain upright if she took her arms from either side of her, so she urged her sister to lean forward. Wendy stuck one arm beneath the tent to keep Cait from tipping forward, and pounded almost mercilessly on her back.

Rory gasped.

"I have to," Wendy said. "Sometimes you just can't be gentle."

At last they found success. Even as she listened to the necessary coughing, though, Rory heard how bad it was. Her sister's congestion was worsening. From the sound of it, she might have begun to drown.

And all of this might be for naught.

Wendy kept at it, though, until Cait's breathing sounded clear. Rory could easily imagine that her sister's back must be bruised, but there was no other option.

At last Cait sagged back against her, and they were able to get her to drink some hot tea, which made her cough some more. This time the coughing sounded normal.

They all ate quickly, their food heated over a second fire. Cait even swallowed a few mouthfuls and asked for more tea. A good sign? God, Rory hoped so.

They packed up as quickly as they could, tying Cait once again to Chase with bungee cords. Rory offered to carry her, but he shook his head.

"I'm used to the altitude. I know Cait doesn't weigh much, but it might be too much for you right now. We don't need you to get pulmonary edema."

More hiking. More snowy stops. An occasional

clearing where the going became even harder with deeper snow.

Rory lost all sense of time, all sense of how far they had traveled. She had become an automaton, awakening from the daze only when Cait needed tending.

At some point she realized that the day was waning. The sun poked through a few times, and once, as they approached a clearing, she could see the lengthening shadows.

One more day of meds for Cait. And they might prove useless.

But she had wearied too much now to even feel the fear. Numbness took over and she let it.

It was a small blessing.

All of a sudden, when she was sure that night was close to overtaking them, Chase froze.

"Stop. Listen."

Rory obeyed, wondering what he wanted them to hear. At first she heard nothing at all except the stirring of the treetops in a wind that couldn't reach them down here. Not a bird call, not a snapping twig.

Then, slowly, she caught snatches of a humming sound. A plane? She hardly dared believe it.

Chase looked at Yuma. "Now?"

He nodded. "Let them know our general area. We'll have to press on a little longer in hopes of finding a clearing."

Rescue? Could it be? Rory almost collapsed to the ground, but found some last reserve of strength to keep herself upright.

Chase fumbled at a bag that had been hanging at his belt and brought out the flare gun. He loaded it with quick efficiency, then looked up for an opening.

There were plenty. The woods had thinned here for some reason. He waited.

"Why are you waiting?" Rory asked.

"Because we have a better chance of being seen if the plane is coming this way."

She hadn't thought of that. Despair started warring with hope inside her. What if it was some normal flight, and came no closer?

She listened as hard as she could. Chase kept turning his head this way and that as if trying to locate the sound.

Rory hoped she wasn't imagining it, but the engine seemed to be approaching them.

Suddenly, Chase lifted his arm and fired. Rory tipped her head back, watching the flare rise until it burst into bright red flame, then rise even higher. It seemed to hang in the air above their heads, high, but maybe not high enough. Then, all too soon, it began to fall, growing dimmer as it did so.

Oh, God, what if it hadn't been seen?

"Let's keep moving," Yuma said.

"But they'll know we're here," Rory protested.

"If they saw that flare, we're not going to get so far that they won't see the next one and locate us. We're going to need a clearing to be rescued anyway."

So they stumbled on, but more slowly this time. Rory was certain she wasn't the only one straining her ears, listening for the plane engine over the muffled sounds of their breathing and their footfalls.

Another personal eternity passed for her before Chase waved them all to a stop again.

Rory held her breath. Then she heard it. The engine's buzz was coming closer. "Oh, God," she breathed brokenly.

Chase took a couple of steps and fired another flare.

Once again all their hopes rose with it.

Even as high as it went, she thought she could hear it hiss and sizzle. The plane engine was still at some distance.

And night was encroaching steadily. Too late. Oh, God, too late. Her heart fell to her shoes, and a tear leaked out to freeze on her cold cheek.

Then, like the cavalry in the last minutes of an old Western, the sound grew louder. Steadily. Closer and closer.

And then, to her amazement, through the treetops she saw a plane fly over, low, almost too low, and as it did it waggled its wings.

Yuma let out a loud, "Yeehaw! Those are our guys!"

Dulled by fatigue, Rory hardly dared believe it. "They found us?"

"They found us," Chase said. "But we still have to get through the night."

"Why?" God, she felt like a dullard. She suspected that she already knew the answer, but they wouldn't come. The cold had seeped into her brain.

"Because they can't come in the dark, and there are still too many trees. But they've marked where we are. We'll find a clearing, and they'll be back at first light."

"That's right," Yuma agreed. "First light. And they won't quit until they have us."

She stumbled forward to check on Cait again. What she heard made her wonder if morning would be soon enough.

Chapter 10

Yuma led them to a small clearing. It wasn't huge, but he judged it large enough.

They tucked Cait into the shelter of a huge boulder while they made a camp with the survival blankets. Once again, dull as she was feeling from the cold and altitude, she was amazed at the things Chase had stowed on his plane, things he had brought with them.

Duct tape joined the pieces of survival blanket and taped them to pine boughs to make a lean-to. A couple more of them made a groundcover.

"Why do you carry so many of these?" she asked him.

"In case. They fold up to almost nothing, so why shortchange myself? I always figured if I was in a situation like this with passengers, I'd hate myself for being cheesy."

"I'm glad you're not cheesy."

He flashed her a smile.

She had started to stumble, but refused to give in as she helped gather wood from the forest for a fire to keep them warm overnight. The lean-to arrangement with a fire at the mouth promised as much coziness as they could hope for, short of a cave, and she didn't think any of them were about to hunt for one.

Finally, Chase told her to climb under the shelter and take care of Cait.

At least he hadn't pointed out that, unlike the rest of them, her stamina seemed to be failing. She was ashamed of that, then told herself not to be silly. She wasn't used to the cold, she'd given her warmest clothes to her sister, and the altitude wasn't helping, either.

"How high are we?" she asked.

"Over six thousand feet. That's enough to make any flatlander weary. You need some liquids, hot ones, and some warmth. You'll come back quickly."

She hoped so. Falling apart at this stage seemed ludicrous.

This time they built a bigger fire. The tent captured its heat and reflected its light into a wonderful bright yellow glow. Cait awoke again as they started boiling water, and Rory used a pine bough to sweep the steam into the tent.

Soon Cait was coughing again—deep, racking coughs that frightened Rory as much as they relieved her. She gave Cait medicine, and more hot soup and tea, and even received a smile for her efforts.

Chase brought her soup of her own, and some warmed-up mash of ready-to-heat foods he'd had on the plane. Ambrosia.

They made cowboy coffee, too, in the chafing dish, and she ignored the occasional coffee ground.

"Adds body," Chase said to her with a wink.

Weary and worried though she was, she managed a small laugh in response.

Cait woke up again and seemed a little brighter. Considering that they were keeping hot water steaming just inside the lean-to, near the fire, Rory thought that might be helping her sister revive. More coughing, which was good, and then a request for more tea.

"We're going to get out of here in the morning," Rory told her as she helped her hold the cup. "They know where we are now. You'll be in a hospital soon."

Cait wrinkled her nose, and astonished her with a flash of humor. "That's *good* news?"

Rory obligingly laughed again, although she was terrified of the hours between now and then. Cait felt feverish—no mistaking it. She was far too warm for it to be explained by the heat in the lean-to. In fact, the lean-to was warm only by comparison with the dark world beyond it.

But at least her own earlobes felt as if they were thawing.

"Rory?"

She turned at once to her sister, who was now lying cocooned on the groundcover. "Yes?"

"I want you to know something."

"What's that?"

"I know I haven't been awake much. I know I upset you when I say I don't want to fight anymore." Cait paused, panting a bit, trying to get her breath. "But I want you to know...I know you've done all you can. More than most people would."

"Shh... You need your breath."

Cait gave a little shake of her head. "I know, Rory.

I want you to know that. I know how much…you love me. I love you, too."

Rory felt tears prick her eyes, even as dread squeezed her heart. Surely Cait wasn't trying to say goodbye? Cait couldn't possibly believe she'd be gone before morning. Every cell in Rory wanted to scream a fierce denial. *No, you're not taking her,* she shouted inwardly. *Not now, not after all of this.* God, the cruelty of it at this point would be beyond bearing. All this fight, all this struggle, all for naught? No way. *No way.*

Instead of giving voice to her terror and anger, she managed a calm response. "You can tell me all this once we get you to the hospital and you can breathe again, okay?"

"Okay." A sigh. Then so softly Rory almost missed it, "I *do* want to live."

They took watches again that night to keep the fire burning high while ensuring that it didn't burn their tent. Sleep wasn't easy, but it no longer mattered to Rory.

She wrapped herself around Cait on one side, and was touched when Chase wrapped himself around them both from the other side.

"A sandwich is warmer," he said, then reached for and held her hand. "You're cold."

"I'll be warm tomorrow."

"More coffee or tea?"

"When we next take care of Cait." Then she whispered, "One more night."

"We'll make it."

"I think we will, thanks to you and your Boy Scout motto. You were prepared for everything."

"Not quite." He sighed. "But maybe enough."

"Oh, definitely enough. All these survival blankets. Duct tape. Flare gun. Food, candles... Chase, if my portable office in Mexico was half as well-stocked as that plane, I'd brag."

"You don't fly. You're firmly planted on the ground. Besides, you're talking to a guy who was given survival training by his former employer. They taught me enough, setting me free with only what I could carry on a fighter with me. I developed quite a list of things that were portable and would make surviving easier."

"I can see that. Coffee even."

"Hey, nothing short of Armageddon can separate a navy flier from his coffee."

She smiled in the dark. "Thank you."

"Thank me when you get to Minnesota," he said gruffly.

"I will."

"Good. So are you going to stay with your sister during her treatment?"

"As much as I can. I'm hoping to be there for the whole thing, but business may rear up." At this point, though, business didn't seem to matter at all. Not even wild horses were going to drag her away until she knew Cait was getting better. Or until it was over. The last thought caught in her throat, tightening it. She swallowed hard and pushed the notion of failure away. She couldn't, wouldn't, allow herself to think of it.

"Yeah, business has a way of doing that, doesn't it? Well, don't be surprised if you find me standing outside your portable office one day. I got wings, lady. Or I will again soon."

Rory's chest ached with an impending sense of loss. Were they saying goodbye? It certainly sounded like it.

If so, she wanted it to be a good one. "I also need to thank you for teaching me some things."

"I didn't teach you a damn thing, darlin'."

"You did." She didn't feel like exposing herself right then, though. She was exhausted, worried and very much on edge. "You made me think some things through, and in the process I learned something about myself."

"I could say the same. Watching you with Cait…well, let's just say I know I've been missing something. And that I've been making bad choices. But I told you that."

"Yes." She fell silent then, lost in wandering thoughts, all of which came back to the same place. When she left here tomorrow for Minnesota, she was going to be leaving friends behind. Worse, she was going to be leaving Chase behind. She was sure he was teasing about showing up at her office someday. It was just a kind, joking thing to say to lighten this last awful night.

He'd done a lot of that, she realized. In a quiet, no-horn-tooting sort of way, he'd shouldered responsibilities, among them helping her to stay strong. He'd let her lean on him, and taught her that leaning was not necessarily a bad thing.

Her life was going to be poorer without him.

In fact, it was going to be downright empty. Saving her sister was paramount, of course. Top of the list, no question. But saying farewell to Chase was going to be extremely hard.

She truly wished she didn't have to.

Chase's thoughts were following a similar line: *no future in this*. He couldn't believe he'd tipped over the brink of caring in less than two days. He'd never let himself really care for a woman before. Ever.

Yet this one had somehow wormed her way into a special place. He guessed that made him a fool, because tomorrow or the next day she'd be on her way to Minnesota with her sister, and from there to Mexico. He might joke about having wings, but he knew better.

They'd shared an intense time, everything heightened because of the crash and Cait's condition. He wouldn't have believed it if she said she cared for him, and he couldn't believe his own lying heart.

But as the night hours dragged by on leaden feet, he knew that he was about to lose something. He wasn't exactly sure what, but he could sense the impending loss.

The best thing to do, he decided, was to make sure she left without feeling that she owed him anything. Make it clear that the last two days had created no ties that couldn't snap in an instant.

He had to let her go free of any sense of obligation or debt, because he didn't want her that way. He'd rather lose her than risk that. So he'd cut her loose tomorrow. If she chose to look him up later, that would be different, but for now he had to do what was best.

Best for *both* of them. God, he was going to hate himself come tomorrow.

Thoughts of separation didn't last long. A few hours later, Cait's breathing worsened noticeably. The rasping woke Rory from a doze.

"Chase? Wendy?"

In an instant, both were squatting over Cait.

"It sounds like she's drowning." Instinctively, Rory pulled Cait up into a sitting position. Never, ever in her life had she heard someone sound like this. Cait didn't even wake up, not even when jerked upright.

Chase swore. He went to get the dish full of steaming water and cussed again. "It's dry. I'll get some snow."

Yuma was up now, too, pulling on his boots. "I'll build up the fire."

Rory wrapped her arm around her sister and pounded her back. What else could she do?

"Stop for a second," Wendy said. She pulled away blankets, unzipped Cait's jacket and pressed her ear to the woman's chest. "She's filling up."

"Oh, God," Rory said faintly. "Oh, God."

Wendy didn't offer any false hope. Not a shred of it. "I need a hot, wet cloth," she said.

Rory didn't hesitate. She pulled off her sweater and crawled out into the snow. She pushed as much snow into the fabric as she could then crawled over to the fire. She didn't even feel the night air's bite.

As soon as the snow melted into the sweater and the fabric grew hot, she scooted over to Wendy.

Wendy took it and stuffed it inside Cait's jacket, covering her chest with it before rezipping the parka.

Then she pounded Cait's back again.

Cait's eyes fluttered opened. She drew a shallow, ragged, wet breath, then coughed. It almost sounded like a barking seal. "I'm sorry."

"Hush," Rory said sharply. "Just cough, dammit."

Cait tried again, but it sounded both weak and far too tight.

The light suddenly brightened and Rory turned her head to see Yuma throwing more dry pine branches on the fire. Chase was already hovering over the bowl of snow, and she could see steam starting to rise.

When it was good and hot, he grabbed it with his

gloved hands and brought it to them, duck-walking beneath their shelter. He didn't set it down but held it directly under Cait's chin.

"Breathe, Cait," Rory begged. "As deeply as you
can."

Chase looked over his shoulder. "Yuma, get that
other pot out of the duffel. Boil more water."

"You got it."

Cait's breathing was so shallow that Rory despaired
that she could draw enough steam into her lungs. "Cait,
please, try. Inhale it."

Cait opened her mouth and drew a breath. It was a
little one, but Rory could see steam drifting toward and
into her mouth.

"Another one, Cait."

Wendy pounded some more, but no cough emerged.
She looked at Rory over Cait's head. "We're going to
have to keep this up until the 'copter gets here."

"Then I will."

"No," said Chase. "*We* will."

"I must have fallen asleep," Rory said. "Oh, God,
how could I have slept and not heard this?"

"Rory." Wendy's voice was firm. "Given her condition I told you this could be sudden. You probably heard
it the minute it got worse. We've been getting her to
cough regularly. It's all we could do then. Now we do
what we can do nonstop until rescue gets here."

After a moment, Rory nodded. What else could she
do?

Chase switched the steaming bowls. Wendy pulled
the wet sweater out again and told Rory to reheat it.

Though it seemed like forever, probably a half hour
passed before Cait had her first productive cough. Then

she drew a deeper breath, though not deep enough, and sounded a bit looser.

"Good," said Wendy with evident satisfaction. "One of you guys get some sleep. We only need three of us to take care of this."

But nobody slept. Nobody even tried. The steaming-bowl brigade continued. Yuma took over heating the sweater for Rory, and in between times gathered more wood for the fire.

Little by little, Cait's breathing improved.

Rory looked at Wendy. "What about when she's on the chopper?"

"They can give her plenty of oxygen. They also have other stuff. Don't worry about that."

"Okay."

Never had she been more out of her element than in these long night hours. She barely felt it when Chase touched her shoulder, barely noticed that her lack of response caused him to draw back a bit.

Only one thing mattered: Cait.

Chase felt her withdrawal as rejection. All he'd tried to do was offer silent comfort, and she'd acted like he wasn't even there. Good. That would make his task easier.

In the meantime, he wanted nothing more than to ensure that Cait survived to be evacuated. He wanted it for Rory most of all, but he wanted it for himself, too.

Because there were some burdens that might be too heavy to carry. He wanted Cait to live. He didn't want to feel responsible for killing her.

And he would if they didn't get her out of here alive, and get her past the pneumonia.

The rest of the night he ferried water and listened

hopefully as Cait coughed and struggled to draw deeper breaths. Little by little, she seemed to improve.

And then, just before the first pale light of dawn began to overtake the fire's light, she had a coughing fit he thought might kill her all by itself.

When it passed, she sagged against her sister, and at long last drew a deep breath. And then another.

"Tea?" he asked.

Cait nodded weakly.

He went to the pot that was heating by the fire, made the tea with plenty of sugar, and passed the cup to Rory.

Then he rose and left the lean-to, to walk around the clearing's edge.

If God had any mercy, he thought, that woman would survive and get her trial on the new drug. And if any of that mercy was left over, he hoped he could find a way to cut the tie with Rory. For good.

Neither of them needed this. It was born of an artificial closeness. He gave himself another dozen or so arguments, absolutely none of which he believed, but what the hell.

It was going to hurt, but not for long. She hadn't been in his life for enough time to leave a permanent scar.

He only wished he believed that.

As soon as it was light enough for visual flight rules over these mountains, he heard a plane engine coming their way again. He stood in the middle of the clearing, flare gun ready.

"Build up that fire, Yuma?"

"I already am."

When it sounded close enough, Chase sent up his last flare. They damn well better see it.

Five breathless minutes later, the plane soared over them and waggled its wings. They had been sighted.

Now it would be only a matter of time before the chopper arrived.

Reluctantly, he turned back to the lean-to. Cait was still drinking tea. Rory looked at him, something he couldn't define in her gaze, then her attention slipped away.

He'd definitely been relegated to the forgotten. And he was going to make damn sure he stayed there somehow.

For both their sakes.

A half hour later the helicopter arrived, emblazoned with a red cross and blue lettering on white that identified it as a medical evacuation chopper. It hovered as low as it could without landing on the snow or clipping the trees, its roar deafening.

It lowered an EMT to them immediately, then lifted a bit, waiting. He greeted Wendy and Yuma with quick hugs while Wendy filled him in on Cait.

Within five minutes, after he spoke through his headset to the chopper, he was lifted again. Then down came a basket stretcher.

Her heart pounding madly, Rory helped settle Cait into it and strap her in. When Wendy was satisfied, she made a winding motion with her hand and the stretcher began to lift, swaying a bit, but far steadier than Rory would have believed possible.

Then Cait vanished into the door of the chopper.

Wendy leaned close to Rory. "They can take only one more person on this trip. They're sending down a harness for you."

"You should go," Rory said, panic stabbing at her. "You know how to navigate it all, get her help faster."

Wendy grabbed her forearm. "Hang in there. You know as much about her condition as I do, and when that thing lands at the hospital, there's going to be no hesitation in beginning treatment. Plus, you know her doctors, right?"

Rory nodded, looking up.

"You know more of the important stuff than I do, and there's an EMT onboard right now," Wendy said. "You don't need an extra one."

Only then did Rory admit that she didn't want to let her sister out of her sight. She was afraid something would happen and she wouldn't be there. She couldn't bear the thought.

She looked toward Chase. He nodded, his expression cool. "Good luck. I hope it all turns out well for you."

Woodenly, she allowed Wendy and Yuma to buckle her into the waiting harness. He hadn't even asked her to let him know how it came out.

She wondered if she could stand anymore, because her heart was cracking again, this time because of Chase.

Then a flicker of fury saved her. She read the farewell in his eyes, in the dismissive tone. In the way he wished her luck, and didn't say anything about seeing her later. She felt used. She looked him square in the eye and spoke coldly.

"Have a nice life."

Then the winch lifted her to whatever the future held.

The local hospital put her in a bed next to Cait's in the emergency room. The oxygen seemed to be brightening her color, and Rory hardly tore her gaze from her sister as people checked her out for exposure, pumped fluids into her, insisted that she eat.

Cait was unconscious again, but the E.R. personnel lifted the burden from Rory's shoulders. The E.R. doctors spoke to Cait's doctors in Seattle, and came in to tell Rory that a treatment plan had been made. They were going to treat the pneumonia immediately with powerful antibiotics and decongestants.

She watched again and again as they forced Cait to cough.

Then a nurse came to tell her that they had arranged medical transport to Minnesota the next day. Cait would still get into the trial as long as her pneumonia showed improvement by tomorrow or the next day.

By late afternoon, Cait's breathing improved. Hope alone was enough to allow Rory to lie back and give it all into the hands of the medical people. Not long after that, they released her and she followed Cait up to ICU, where she remained in a chair beside her sister's bed.

"How are you doing?"

Wendy's voice drew her out of numb preoccupation and she looked up. "Okay. She's breathing better."

"I can hear that."

"They say her tests show no organ damage, so that's good."

Wendy nodded. "I heard. And she's still going for the trial."

"Yes."

"Then we succeeded."

"Thanks to you and Yuma. And Chase." Chase who hadn't bothered to come by even once to see how Cait was doing, how *she* was doing.

Wendy hesitated. "You and Chase…"

"It was nothing. Forget it. I have."

And that was probably the biggest lie she had ever told.

Chapter 11

Rory was coming out of the hospital on a cold Minnesota afternoon, planning to get a decent meal somewhere besides the hospital cafeteria.

A familiar voice brought her up short.

"Howdy, stranger."

She turned slowly and saw Chase standing there on the sidewalk looking oddly awkward. At least for Chase. He smiled uncertainly.

All the pain she'd refused to allow herself to feel rose up in a tidal wave and transformed into anger. "What are you doing here? Not having a nice life?"

With that she turned and started to storm away. He'd hurt her worse than she had realized until later, and she wasn't going to let him hurt her again. No way.

But he caught up with her. "I wanted to see how Cait is doing."

She resisted answering him, but finally said shortly, "Much better."

"Really?"

She kept walking.

"Rory, look. I owe you a date."

"Like I care."

"Then call it lunch. I need to talk with you."

"No, you don't. You made that clear over the last couple of months."

"I was an ass. Does that help?"

"And you're not being one now?"

"God, I hope not."

Somehow that got through to her. She glanced at him, and realized that his face still had the power to tug at her heart. "Lunch," she finally agreed grudgingly. "Not a date."

"Fine." Another half smile. "Where?"

"There's a place up here that offers a better menu than the hospital cafeteria."

"Sounds perfect."

It wasn't an upscale restaurant by any means, basically a diner with a counter and booths and food that didn't try to match some dietitian's view of hell.

They slid into a booth facing each other, and said little until after they ordered.

"So she's really improving," Chase said when the waitress walked away.

"It's amazing," Rory said, and her voice cracked a bit. "For the first time since I came home, doctors are saying hopeful things to me. All I heard before was that I'd better prepare myself. That she only had weeks or at most a few months. Now I'm actually hearing references to when she finishes this treatment. There's a future again."

"Thank God." His words were clearly heartfelt, and despite herself she warmed a bit toward him. "Long term?"

"She'll probably never be cured. Few cancers really are, I guess. But she can have this treatment again if necessary. The doctors are thrilled by how she's responding. So am I. Chase, she's smiling again. Eating. Starting to talk about things she wants to do."

"That's wonderful. That must make you feel wonderful."

"It does, obviously. I hardly dared hope."

"I know. But you fought for her like a tiger."

She hesitated. "You helped."

"Not much. I'm the guy who brought us down on a mountainside."

"Safely," she reminded him. "Did you find out what happened?"

"A comedy of errors that almost wasn't a comedy, if you get my drift. A handful of things went wrong because mechanics missed something, or failed to do something exactly right. No single one of them would have been catastrophic, but put them all together that's what they became. Oh, and you'll love this."

"What?"

"The beacon wasn't working at all. That freaking expensive piece of equipment I had installed so our location could be pinpointed in a crash failed. I guess that wasn't installed right, either."

"Maybe you need to find a new mechanic."

"I'm not sure, but some heads are going to roll."

She nodded. "So you get your new plane?"

"I flew here on it."

"That was fast."

He shrugged. "That overhaul was done by the plane's

manufacturer. Once the preliminary report came from the NTSB, they couldn't give me a replacement fast enough."

"I'm glad you're back in business."

Silence fell again. Their sandwiches were served, both of them thick and meat-laden.

"How about your business?" he asked after they'd eaten a few mouthfuls.

"I'm managing it long-distance. Thank God for the telephone and the internet."

"That's good."

Another silence, this one more awkward. What was she doing here? This was worse than ripping a sticky bandage off a wound. She could feel barely formed scabs shrieking.

"Rory…" He hesitated. "I've had some time to think. I need some time with you. To talk. To figure out stuff. I didn't want to be a bastard, but I was. Please. Can you spare me some time?"

She hesitated, realizing that she wanted to hear what he had to say, regardless of how difficult it might be to hear. The way they had parted had given her no closure at all. She needed some closure on her episode with him, just so she could live with herself.

Especially now that the future existed once again, with Cait's improvement.

"All right," she said finally. "I'll go back to the hospital and tell Cait I'm going to be away for a while."

"Thank you."

They talked casually thereafter. He told her more about Wendy and Yuma, and how they were doing. "They wanted to come along to see Cait. I told them next trip."

Rory caught her breath. "You believed that strongly that she was going to get better?"

"If she's anything like her sister, I figured her for a fighter."

"She almost lost that fight."

"I know. Don't lose yours. Not for any reason."

What did he mean by that? she wondered as they walked back to the hospital. As they rounded a corner, the icy winter wind snatched at them and she almost lost her breath. He reached to hold her elbow, to steady her, and she didn't pull away.

Soon enough, she told herself, he'd be gone for good, and she could start growing the scabs again. Put the bandages back in place. Get on with life.

Cait waved at them through the glass that separated her from the world until her immune system was restored. When Rory said she was thinking about being away for a few hours, Cait waved a hand.

"Go. For heaven's sake, get out of here and breathe something that doesn't smell like iodine."

Chase laughed. "You *do* sound better."

"I am. Now go—both of you."

"Where are you staying?" Chase asked as they reached the lobby. "I don't really want to talk in public. It'll make me nervous."

"But it might keep me from yelling."

He gave her a smile that at once looked a bit pained, yet reached his eyes with real humor. "I deserve it. If you want to yell, I'll listen."

The cab ride was short, and soon they were in her hotel room, a nice enough place but nothing special. She only slept here and worked from a laptop on the table. There were two chairs, though, and once they'd doffed their jackets, they sat.

"Okay," she said. "I'm listening."

"First of all, maybe I'm an ass—actually, I know I am—but I felt you wouldn't want anything to continue between us."

"And you got that idea where?"

"From the way you acted in the last few hours. So I decided, given that everything that had happened occurred partly because we were under extreme pressure…" He paused. "Let me find another way to phrase that. I wanted us both to have space, to see if what happened meant anything."

"I might remind you," she said a bit sarcastically, "that you were the one who said you really got to know a person fast in those conditions."

"I did. And I still believe it. But that doesn't mean it's anything that can go past that."

She couldn't argue that, she supposed. They had been in a crucible, and while it might reveal their true characters, it didn't mean they could handle normal life together. Especially with both of them being at opposite ends of the world half the time. She sighed.

"I didn't want to hurt you," he said. "I was trying to be smart."

"Maybe you were." The words were heavy with reluctance, because as she looked at him now, she realized that she had feelings for him that had extended well beyond those few days.

He fell silent, a kind of sadness settling over his face. "Maybe so. Maybe that's how you feel. Maybe you're right."

"I didn't exactly say that." And she had just exposed herself. Clenching her hands, she waited for the bomb to drop.

"No, you didn't." He leaned forward, passed his hand

over his face. "Man, I could screw up falling off a log. Look. What I'm saying is, I've spent the last few months telling myself to forget you. I can't. I just can't. For the first time in my life, I can't just walk away. You'll have to send me away. And if you don't, I'm not going to be greedy. I'm just going to ask you to give us a chance."

"A chance for what?" But her heart was beating heavily now, rising with hope that only a few short weeks ago she had feared she would never feel again. Cait was improving. Now Chase was suggesting…suggesting what exactly?

"A chance to see if we can build something together. I want to date you. I don't care if I have to fly to the jungles of Mexico as often as I can manage and eat tortillas by candlelight while battling mosquitoes and other critters. I just want us to try. Is that possible?"

For the last few months she'd been telling herself that she wouldn't care if Chase Dakota fell off a cliff. She'd been telling herself lies. She knew that now, as tears pricked at her eyes, as her heart began to soar. Hope. So much hope. It overwhelmed her.

"Rory? If it's not possible just shake your head and tell me to go."

She'd walked away from him once. She didn't have the strength to do it again. She'd never be able to live with herself if she did.

"Stay," she said finally, a whisper.

He let out a whoop and jumped up. "Really?"

"Really."

Suddenly he was on his knees in front of her, cradling her face in his hands. "I admire everything I've seen of you. This whole time I've been beating myself up for not at least trying. I never before met a woman who reached the places you reach inside me. They've been cold, empty places for too long."

She knew exactly what he meant, but it was getting so hard to breathe. Emotions were overwhelming her, her protective shell was cracking, and it hurt worse than anything except her fear for Cait.

No more talk, she thought. "Shut up, Chase."

Then, as he started to pull back, she leaned in and kissed him.

An instant later his arms surrounded her, holding her so tightly it almost hurt. His tongue sought hers, instantly lifting her to that place only he had ever taken her.

The room spun, and she realized that he had lifted her and carried her to the bed. Then he laid her down, standing over her, smiling. Absolutely smiling, the most beautiful expression she had ever seen.

He looked so powerful. She wasn't used to seeing him without the bulk of winter clothing, and she liked what she saw. He was strong, lean, tall. And he was impatient. He pulled his clothes off as if they were still in the frigid plane, as if he couldn't risk getting cold before he dived into her warmth.

But he was gentler with her, far gentler. He unwrapped her as if she were a fragile gift, as if he wanted to delay the moment of discovery just a little longer.

She felt a fleeting shyness, because before they had made love in the dark, and this room was bright with winter light pouring in the window. But the way he looked at her drove that shyness away.

"You're beautiful," he said. "Perfect."

"No…"

"Oh, hush, just accept the compliment."

That startled a giggle out of her, and shyness took

flight. Then he took her on another flight with him. Lying beside her, the cold no longer a concern, he drank her in with his eyes, then studied her with his hands.

She could not long remain still. She turned toward him, reciprocating as she hadn't been able to before.

She found all his muscled hollows and hardness with her hands, memorizing the dry warmth of his skin, the way he flexed on her touches, loving it each time she drew a moan from him.

They didn't have to be quiet this time, and soon her moans were melding with his as they hungrily explored each other. No place was too secret to be discovered by hands or mouth.

The heat built in her, along with that wonderful ache. And when she felt that she couldn't bear to wait another minute, he made her wait longer.

Until, finally, his name was an imploring chant that emerged on moan after moan.

The world spun again, and she found herself straddling him, his staff hard against her most sensitive places. His eyes were heavy-lidded as he looked up at her, a smile at the corners of his mouth.

He reached up, cupping both her breasts at once, tormenting her nipples with his thumbs. Helpless, she leaned down until he could take one into his mouth. Each time he sucked strongly, she felt it throughout every inch of her body, and between her legs the throbbing ache grew.

She was in charge, the way she liked to be. The thought flitted across her mind, recognizing the gift he was giving her, but was immediately lost in the rising drumbeat of passion.

At last she reared up, and looked down to where their bodies almost joined. So close, yet so far.

"Wait," he managed huskily. He reached for the bed-side table. She saw the foil packets immediately and grabbed one, tearing it open.

Then she did something she had never done before: she rolled the protection onto his staff, finding it one of the sexiest things she had ever done, especially when he writhed in response and deep sounds of pleasure escaped him.

She discovered that she enjoyed teasing him, and making him wait. Then, almost euphoric in her pleasure, she gave in to her body's demands. Rising, she impaled herself on his manhood. All the way. Deeply.

And as their centers met, she threw back her head and closed her eyes, savoring the fullness, loving the exquisite, intimate contact.

She didn't move immediately. No, she held them suspended that way, propping herself on her elbows and she came down onto his chest. With her mouth she found one of his small nipples, and discovered that teasing them and sucking them pleased him just as it pleased her when he did it to her.

Delight speared her, for now she had a new way to delight him.

But at last, at long last, she couldn't hold back the tide anymore.

Her hips moved in a helpless, ancient rhythm. She felt him grip her rear, keeping her close, his touch heightening her desire.

Together, all barriers gone, they climbed their way to the stars.

Later, much later, they showered together, then dressed.

"I need to go see Cait," she said.

"I'll go with you."

"I'd like that."

When they were just about ready to put on their outerwear, he stopped her, taking her hand. "I want you to consider something."

"What's that?"

"After Cait gets out of here...well, where is she going to go? You said her husband left her."

"I haven't gotten that far," she admitted.

"Then I have a suggestion. She can stay with me while you have to be in Mexico. We'll be a family."

Stunned, she plopped down on the messed-up bed. "Chase, do you know what you're saying?"

"I think so. Okay, she needs to see doctors. I can provide transport. I can keep her company when she has to be here and you're away."

"But...but that's a *commitment!*"

"I know. And I know how big it is."

"But you said..." Her mind was reeling. Her heart was leaping.

"I know what I said. Call it my wedge. What I really want is for us to do more than try. And I like your sister. I know exactly what I'm volunteering for here. Trust me. I've seen it."

She believed him. His generosity finally broke the dam, and tears began to roll down her cheeks.

"You'd feel better, wouldn't you, to know she's not alone when you're away. That someone who cares about you also is caring for her."

"My God..." She couldn't speak through her tight throat.

"I'm not just going to try, Rory. I'm going to do my damnedest to make this work for all three of us."

She stared mutely at him through blurry eyes.

"Rory? Did I say something wrong?"

"No." She swallowed. "Oh, no. You just said the most beautiful thing in the world."

He began to smile. "Then let me add, I'm pretty damn sure I'm in love with you. And on my honor, I've never ever said that to anyone before."

"I...I'm in love with you, too," she admitted.

He reached for her then, holding her close, murmuring in her ear. "We'll make it work," he vowed. "We will make it all work. I want marriage. I want Cait to live with us. Kids are negotiable, depending on how you feel about it. But one thing I swear, and that's that I can't live my life without you."

She hugged him back, squeezing her eyes against tears of joy. "I love you, too. I couldn't bear the thought that I'd never see you again. I couldn't."

"So start planning on permanence. I let you go once. I'm not going to do it again."

The joy that filled her became incandescent. "I want kids."

"Good. Put them on your calendar. You can even add a picket fence if you want."

The tears were still falling, but she laughed. It felt so good to laugh.

"I love you, Rory."

"I love you, Chase."

And an hour later, when they stood looking at Cait in her isolation room, they held up their linked hands.

Cait, who no longer looked as fragile as a dandelion puff, grinned. It was a wide, happy grin, and she applauded.

For the first time ever, Rory knew that life could be perfect. Oh, not always, but every now and then.

And right now it was pure perfection.

* * * * *

ROMANTIC
SUSPENSE

COMING NEXT MONTH

Available September 27, 2011

You can find more information on upcoming Harlequin® titles, free excerpts and more at **www.HarlequinInsideRomance.com**.

REQUEST YOUR FREE BOOKS!
2 FREE NOVELS PLUS 2 FREE GIFTS!

ROMANTIC
SUSPENSE

Sparked by Danger, Fueled by Passion.

YES! Please send me 2 FREE Harlequin® Romantic Suspense novels and my 2 FREE gifts (gifts are worth about $10). After receiving them, if I don't wish to receive any more books, I can return the shipping statement marked "cancel." If I don't cancel, I will receive 4 brand-new novels every month and be billed just $4.49 per book in the U.S. or $5.24 per book in Canada. That's a saving of at least 14% off the cover price! It's quite a bargain! Shipping and handling is just 50¢ per book in the U.S. and 75¢ per book in Canada.* I understand that accepting the 2 free books and gifts places me under no obligation to buy anything. I can always return a shipment and cancel at any time. Even if I never buy another book, the two free books and gifts are mine to keep forever.

240/340 HDN FEFR

Name	(PLEASE PRINT)

Address	Apt. #

City	State/Prov.	Zip/Postal Code

Signature (if under 18, a parent or guardian must sign)

Mail to the **Reader Service:**
IN U.S.A.: P.O. Box 1867, Buffalo, NY 14240-1867
IN CANADA: P.O. Box 609, Fort Erie, Ontario L2A 5X3

Not valid for current subscribers to Harlequin Romantic Suspense books.

Want to try two free books from another line?
Call 1-800-873-8635 or visit www.ReaderService.com.

* Terms and prices subject to change without notice. Prices do not include applicable taxes. Sales tax applicable in N.Y. Canadian residents will be charged applicable taxes. Offer not valid in Quebec. This offer is limited to one order per household. All orders subject to credit approval. Credit or debit balances in a customer's account(s) may be offset by any other outstanding balance owed by or to the customer. Please allow 4 to 6 weeks for delivery. Offer available while quantities last.

Your Privacy—The Reader Service is committed to protecting your privacy. Our Privacy Policy is available online at www.ReaderService.com or upon request from the Reader Service.

We make a portion of our mailing list available to reputable third parties that offer products we believe may interest you. If you prefer that we not exchange your name with third parties, or if you wish to clarify or modify your communication preferences, please visit us at www.ReaderService.com/consumerschoice or write to us at Reader Service Preference Service, P.O. Box 9062, Buffalo, NY 14269. Include your complete name and address.

HRS11B

*Harlequin Romantic Suspense presents the latest book
in the scorching new* KELLEY LEGACY *miniseries
from best-loved veteran series author Carla Cassidy*

*Scandal is the name of the game as the Kelley family fights
to preserve their legacy, their hearts...and their lives.*

Read on for an excerpt from the fourth title
RANCHER UNDER COVER

*Available October 2011
from Harlequin Romantic Suspense*

"Would you like a drink?" Caitlin asked as she walked
to the minibar in the corner of the room. She felt as if she
needed to chug a beer or two for courage.

"No, thanks. I'm not much of a drinking man," he
replied.

She raised an eyebrow and looked at him curiously as she
poured herself a glass of wine. "A ranch hand who doesn't
enjoy a drink? I think maybe that's a first."

He smiled easily. "There was a six-month period in my
life when I drank too much. I pulled myself out of the bottom of a bottle a little over seven years ago and I've never
looked back."

"That's admirable, to know you have a problem and then
fix it."

Those broad shoulders of his moved up and down in
an easy shrug. "I don't know how admirable it was, all I
knew at the time was that I had a choice to make between
living and dying and I decided living was definitely more
appealing."

She wanted to ask him what had happened preceding
that six-month period that had plunged him into the bottom

of the bottle, but she didn't want to know too much about him. Personal information might produce a false sense of intimacy that she didn't need, didn't want in her life.

"Please, sit down," she said, and gestured him to the table. She had never felt so on edge, so awkward in her life.

"After you," he replied.

She was aware of his gaze intensely focused on her as she rounded the table and sat in the chair, and she wanted to tell him to stop looking at her as if she were a delectable dessert he intended to savor later.

*Watch Caitlin and Rhett's sensual saga unfold amidst
the shocking, ripped-from-the-headlines drama
of the Kelley Legacy miniseries in*

RANCHER UNDER COVER

*Available October 2011
only from Harlequin Romantic Suspense,
wherever books are sold.*